The Grandfield Servants

Books of Destiny

***

Olwyn Harris

Published by: Reading Stones Publishing
Helen Brown & Wendy Wood
Woodwendy1982.wixsite.com/readingstones
Cover Design: Olwyn Harris. Some of the cover elements were created using AI Technology. The image of the house, 'But-Har-Gra' was obtained from Wikipedia.org and used under the following licences. Permission is granted to copy, distribute and/or modify this document under the terms of the GNU Free Documentation License, Version 1.2 or any later version published by the Free Software Foundation; with no Invariant Sections, no Front-Cover Texts, and no Back-Cover Texts. A copy of the license is included in the section entitled *GNU Free Documentation License*. And was modified by Olwyn Harris.

For more copies contact the publisher at:

Glenburnie
212 Glenburnie Road
ROB ROY NSW 2360
Mobile: 0422 577 663
Email: Readingstonespublishing@gmail.com

Authors Note

When I was twelve my parents were gifted with a holiday at 'But-Har-Gra' in Sydney. Staying in such an imposing manor-house captured the imagination of this country girl. I was fascinated by the tiled mosaics on the verandah; the grand sweeping polished timber staircase; the thick, wide internal walls that naturally insulated the rooms, so they were cool in summer; the grass tennis courts and the majestic Camphor Laurel trees in the garden. I also remember being told the house had been seconded by the government during WWI and was converted to a war-hospital for injured soldiers, and it became an orphanage in the second world war. The stories of this series are set in a similar house with a similar history. They fulfil a childhood wondering of who might have inhabited such a place, and what might have become of the servants who worked there.

~ Olwyn

Dedication:

For Sue... who embraces destiny with a large heart

Part 1

The Prologue: Grandfield Park

1909

"Now Hillman, be sure Annabelle puts on her new dress: the blue one, with the yellow and white embroidery. And please braid her hair properly. That means not a loose strand is to be seen anywhere. And make sure the ribbon on her hat is pinned discreetly. Do you understand?" Mrs Whitaker frowned severely for emphasis.

Miriam nodded meekly. "Yes Ma'am. Understood."

"There is much to be done, and I do not have time to supervise you. Otherwise having a nursery-governess would be entirely pointless. Your job is to manage Annabelle, to make sure she presents herself appropriately when our guests arrive, like the daughter of Grandfield that she is."

"I understand Ma'am."

"Good. Now, I need to go and talk to Marlie about the hors d'oeuvres. I expect this area to be kept spotless. It is entirely possible there will be wandering feet and eyes when our guests arrive, and I don't want them catching a glimpse of anything that is not as translucent as my pearls or as clear as my crystal decanter set in the parlour. Do you understand?" Without waiting for a response Evaline Whitaker turned on her heel, and then she paused at the door and turned back. "Hillman, I trust you understand that you are here entirely as a favour to your mother's patroness. It would be a shame to send you back because it was not working out."

"Yes Ma'am." Mim swallowed hard on the acid in her throat. The mention of her mother was an unfair card for her to play. It had been over a year, and she still couldn't adjust to the ache in her chest from missing her.

"Just as long as you understand," Mrs Whitaker said again.

Miriam nodded again. "I understand."

'Understanding matters' was a familiar mantra for the grand Mrs Whitaker, with her feathered hats and white gloves. "Well don't stand there Hillman. Hop to it."

That grated... being referred to by her surname without any consideration to her actual name. The name she grew up with had a story... a story her mother would tell her. Her name was Miriam Lily, and her mother's name was Florence, which was the most beautiful city in all the world that was also known as the 'City of Lilies'. Florence was a gem blooming in the hills of Tuscany. Her mother was from there, and she would hug Mim and say, '*Florence and Lilly are practically the same name, because we are the same.*' Her mother was a hopeless romantic, and she was too. Mim put that down to their Italian blood. But it seemed her affectionate namesake was hard to live up to when she was being glared at by the mistress of Grandfield Park, being called 'Hillman'. Names meant a lot to Mim. They were not just nametags; they were part of your identity.

Evaline Whitaker was a force to be reckoned with, like a riptide that would sweep you away and drown you. Mim's brother had drowned because he got caught in an undertow at the beach and he didn't have the strength to fight it. Strange thing was, that a lifeguard told her mother afterwards, that if he had not resisted it, but had gone with it, he may have had the strength to swim ashore later. Mim decided that this was her strategy: go with it. One day she would escape. That is why she would bob and smile and said, "Yes, I understand Ma'am." She was conserving her energy. At some point she would swim out of this riptide and get away.

That meant, her job for now... right this moment, was looking after her charge: Annabelle Whitaker. Anna was eleven. Headstrong. Wilful. A smaller version of her mother, with a quick smile, and a lively, smart turn of phrase with just about everything she said. But Anna had not yet acquired that vinegar taint to pickle her spirit like her mother. Mim's immediate task was to somehow round-up Miss Whitaker and get her ready for this afternoon's tea-party. Another of Mrs Whitaker's mantras echoed in her head, "a well-prepared hostess is a well-regarded hostess". A well-prepared nursery-governess was equally required. Mim scoffed. Mrs Whitaker didn't regard anyone well, regardless of their preparation. And certainly not the invisible ones. Mim was one of the invisible ones and that suited her well enough. What people didn't see became her protection... until she could swim free.

Mim took the dress from the hanger in the wardrobe and placed it carefully on Anna's bed. The frock was pretty with floral embroidery needleworked around the sleeves. The Grandfield seamstress, Mrs Hargrave, was an artist... that was for sure. When Mim started working here, she tried to imagine what it would be like to grow up wearing such dresses, so elegant and fine, even when you are only eleven years old. Mim decided that she certainly would not have dismissed the privilege like this spoilt little girl. With grand naivety, Anna disregarded what it was like to have options.

Mim sighed as she went to find her charge. Then she did a second sweep of the house and grounds. Even Tibbs didn't know where she was. Finally, she went back inside and saw Anna climbing the stairs to the bedroom ahead of her, dragging her feet like she was wadding through mud. Mim watched Anna pause and gaze out the window looking out over the elegant grounds of the Grandfield estate. Suddenly, as if Anna could sense that Mim's apron and cap were near, she turned and flew down the stairs dodging past her in an agile duck and twist. Mim was not able to throw the net quickly enough to snare this flighty bird. "Miss Anna! Your mother needs me to braid your hair!" Mim called after her. "You have to get ready. Come back!"

"Back in a tick! Won't be long," Anna called over her shoulder.

"Miss Anna!" Mim rolled her eyes, sighed, and sunk down to sit in the stairwell. Chasing her would be pointless. She needed to employ ingenuous tactics to have Anna presented in an uncrushed dress, with every bow meticulously tied, not a strand of her fair hair out of place, the toes of her shoes shining like mirrors without any scuffs. Mim sighed and stood up. She looked out the window in the stairwell, and watched Anna quickly climb a tree and disappear into its branches. She deliberated how she would navigate her employer's disfavour when Miss Anna was not ready by the time the guests started to arrive.

* * *

Miraculously, Miss Anna appeared like an apparition. Mim quickly said a prayer of thanks, smartly braided Miss Anna's hair, buttoned her dress, helped buckle her polished shoes and pinned on her hat. There always had to be a hat. Finally, all the required ribbons and bows were tied. And then, just as quickly, Miss Anna disappeared. Mim prayed that Anna would not go climbing trees again and end up tearing her dress. She scanned the wardrobe full of Mrs Hargrave's handiwork. Mim pulled out another Hargrave masterpiece and laid it on the bed, just in case.

Mim was under strict instructions: for the duration of the party, she was to stay out of sight of the guests. This was not a difficult directive to comply with. It would give her time to herself, a luxury that generally only occurred after eight o'clock at night. So, from her nursery look out on her favourite window seat, with a basket of mending in hand, Mim watched the busy preparations at the marquee on the lawn. It had the same feel as when she watched the frantic work of an orchard harvest, as a little girl. She accompanied her dad on seasonal working trips out to the country every year. Even as a youngster, she had to carry baskets of fruit back to the dray and keep track of the tally for the day. It was important work, and it was not long before she ended up being the one to supervise the other kids, so that overworked parents, in their underpaid jobs, could get more of their quota done. She even organised the kids in their own basket-crew; the songs and fun made the hot days and heavy baskets more bearable.

With the eye of a mother-hen, Mim tracked Anna as she placed serviettes carefully at each table setting, under the supervision of Tibbs – the head steward. She raised her eyebrows as she saw Mrs Whitaker float onto the scene like one of the royal family. How would Tibbs justify this gross deviation of protocol if Mrs Whitaker found her princess setting the tables like a common servant? Mim held her breath. This lady's outdated concepts of entitlement were based on living in a bubble called Grandfield Park, and she wondered how long reality would hesitate to put a pin in that bubble. She was glad it was not her responsibility to enlighten Mrs Whitaker to the truth. Mim slowly let out her breath with a shake of her head as she watched Tibbs nod as regally as his employer. Then he gestured to the centrepieces, and with a respectful touch, adjusted a sagging bloom. Mrs Whitaker was satisfied, turned on her heel to avert another more urgent crisis. While Anna was with her "Tibby", Mim had no concerns. Her dress would stay spotless. He had a way with Anna that defied her understanding.

Finally, the boxes that they used to carry the glassware to the tables were cleared away, and Tibbs positioned Anna, practicing the posture and deportment of a Maître-d' near the marquee until her mother arrived to welcome their guests. Now Mim was confident, no one would disturb her, and she was legitimately off duty. She put away the mending, curled up on the window seat, a rug wrapped around her knees, and she reached for her ladies' magazine.

Mim quickly learnt that reading proper books was not deemed a suitable pastime for a nursery governess. It reeked of daring to step outside one's designation. Mim found an easy solution to calm the anxiety that others had about her disturbing inclination. She always had a Ladies' Journal open in her lap, and inside its pages she would rotate through various serious volumes from the library. If anyone ever took the time to notice, they would realise it was impossible to stay engrossed in those journals longer than an afternoon of scanning simple articles and gaudy pictures. It amused Mim that no one ever noticed that her magazines only changed when they became too tattered to effectively serve as a dustcover for her books.

What a joy reading these books was for her. She was able to travel to any number of places. She was able to visit with all sorts of remarkable people and their remarkable lives. She was able to companion others through overwhelming trials and celebrate their exhilarating victories. She could delve into the realms of science, and archelogy, and anthropology without apology. And there was one special book that she read every day. Mim tried to describe what this book meant to her. It was not a novel, nor a philosophical dissertation, nor a reference book. She thought of it as a guidebook. It showed her the way. But even the idea of a 'guidebook' was too cold to describe what it was. Perhaps it was more accurately a love-letter. It was the Bible given to her by her father, and it had been her mother's greatest treasure.

* * *

2.

Sunday was Mim's day off. It was the day when she would dress up, go to the early church service, and sit close to the back, with the covered basket Marlie gave her tucked under the pew. Then she would sneak out, before people were leaving, to visit her father. He lived in a down-sized cottage, at the end of Thredpea Lane... a very shabby little alley. Marlie, from the kitchen, always gave Mim a basket with a loaf of bread, some fruit, or vegetables, like bent carrots or bruised turnips to take home. They were the seconds from the garden, or the market that Marlie insisted she could not use for the main house. And she always included some treats, like a tartlet where the pastry edge had crumbled or a sweet slice, if the knife had slipped and it was cut crooked. Dear Marlie had apologised that she could not legitimately sneak away the good pieces, but she said that it was a waste to throw out "perfectly good food, just because it didn't look perfect." Mim was so grateful for these offerings. They had made such a difference to her father.

She knocked at the weathered old door and called out. "Dad? I'm here." She walked through the passage to the back part of the house where her father was sitting in a worn upholstered chair. She gave him a kiss. "I bought you another book. I found one on horticulture. I have no idea why they would have so many books on gardening... the gardener cannot even read."

He said nothing. His garden now adays, consisted of a bathtub out the back filled with soil. She put it down beside him. "How are you doing Dad? I'm sorry I cannot come more often. But today, I am here all day. I'll do the washing soon... but I will just sit with you for a bit." Mim went to put a log in the stove to boil the kettle. She paused and looked around the cramped living room. Her eyes rested on a couple of picture frames, almost hidden by clutter. A portrait of a wedding, simple and dashing... and a photo of a family gathering taken at a picnic... sunshine and smiles. Mim sighed. Without the photos she would hardly even remember that there really had been better times, even good times.

Tragedy was the tyrant over the Hillman house. And for the life of her, Mim could not remember when Tragedy first came to visit her home, but it came back again, and again, and again, barging in with relentless regularity. There were memories, faded and worn like old postcards: glimpses of living in a nicer house than this little drab cottage on Thredpea Lane; memories of her little brother racing her to the front door with boisterous yahoos to welcome their mother home, coming inside in her crisp, starched uniform. Her father, strong and handsome, was the glue... keeping them all together. He'd serve a simple dinner, before he'd kiss them all goodnight and go out to work the night shift. They were comforting, disturbing, distressing, painful, soothing memories. Sometimes she wondered if they were even real.

The kettle whistled, and she got up to make two very watery cups of tea. "Here, this will warm you up..." His father sipped from the mug, his face tired and aged... older than his actual years, the stubble on his chin was rough and uneven.

He took another sip. "It is good you are here."

"I know Dad. I am sorry I can't... you know, stay during the week."

"I understand work. As did your mother." He swallowed and choked a little.

Mim cleared her throat and took a drink from her mug and then put it down. "Marlie included some eggs in her basket this time. She says that the hens are excited it is Spring and they're laying like crazy, so she had extras. How about I cook some breakfast?"

Her father shrugged and sipped his tea. "Your mother made good tea..." he murmured.

"And you used to make the best breakfasts. I remember you coming home... throwing on the kettle and waking us up by whistling a tune when the kettle started to whistle. It was an amazing way to wakeup... to the smell of fried toast and eggs."

"Huh," he grunted. Mim wasn't sure what he mumbled, but she bounced up to cook their eggs and fry the last of the leftover stale loaf in a bit of lard. They used every last item that Marlie included in these weekly baskets. They couldn't afford to waste anything, even with a fresh delivery of goodies on their table.

Mim cleared away the plates and looked at her father. "So how is your foot?"

"My foot?"

"Yes, your foot. The one on the end of your leg. How is it?"

"It is still on the end of my leg."

"I've been reading about this. It is past the time when the broken bones should have mended, so now we need to get you back on your feet more. We need to strengthen it. Get you to..."

"I can walk you know. I manage all week without you here."

"I know Dad. I know... I just worry. You are not yourself. If you could just get around more... it might be better."

"Don't see how... since I have nowhere to go."

"Oh Dad... it seems you have given up. I need you to be okay. You are my rock." Mim's eyes teared up.

He scoffed. "I think your rock might have turned to mud..."

"I still love him... mud and all. Now show me how you are walking. In fact, let's go for a walk down to the pier."

"That's too far."

"Maybe... but we can start and see how far we get."

"Don't really like the sea..."

"I know Dad... it has memories. But it seems everything has a sad memory attached to it, and if we avoid everything, then we won't be able to go anywhere or do anything. We need to reclaim some of these parts of our life."

"You are like your mother... she always had a positive spin on everything."

"As I remember it... you did too."

"It was a long time ago..."

"Not really... but I am trying to think of something better than leaving you here by yourself for so long. It is not good for you... or me." She reached out her hand, and he held her wrist to help heave himself to his feet. His lips winced as he took his weight. "Do you still strap it with bandages... like I showed you?"

"Yeah. Sometimes..."

"Well, we can't go walking without it wrapped firmly. Here, sit down and let me check it."

He sunk back into the chair with frustration. Mim removed his sock and unwrapped the bandages. She blinked at the smell. "Whew! Do you change them at all?"

"Hard to get at..."

Mim shook her head and scratched her eyebrow. "Okay, let me rewrap it with fresh bandages... and we can try it with that crutch I brought for you. Dad, you have worked hard all your life, and you have never balked at a challenge. This is your days' work right here. Let's get to it."

He nodded, just to keep her satisfied that he was trying. But in all truth, his heart was not in this. Mim buoyantly helped him around the table and navigated towards the door. It was like she was trying to keep him afloat. Down two steps. Out onto the laneway.

As he stepped outside, Mim allowed herself a triumphant smile. "We are going to get to that green door over there, and then see how we go..." Step by step, juggling the awkward crutch, they edged forward. "You're getting a rhythm going now..."

He stared at the green door. One of the manager's offices at the warehouse had a green door. That boss had been as mean as a cut-snake. Huh. Mim was right. Everything... literally every little thing, had a memory attached to it. Why was it that he could only remember the sad things, or the unfair things, or the things that made him mad? Surely there were good memories too. Afterall, his Flo had been the best. And their Walter had been the best. Their life had been the best. Had been. Mim was all that was left of the best.

"Okay," said Mim. "We made it! Did you want to try to get to that crate up ahead and sit down for a bit?"

"The crate it is."

Mim tested the wooden box and helped her father sit down. "We made it. I feel completely exhausted!" she laughed. "Anyone would think it was my foot that had been broken."

"Well at least they didn't chop it off... that was something that they were talking about for a bit. Never seen anyone come through that very well," he said with a scowl.

"Well, it is good that you still have it. See, things are not so bad. You have your foot, and I have a job. We will get there, Dad... you and me. We will."

* * *

"Tibbs? Can I have a word? Please... if you have a moment..."

"Miss Hillman, certainly. What can I do for you?" Tibbs set aside his pen at his desk, and tucked a couple of invoices into the book of accounts before he closed it. He turned to Mim and offered her to take a seat.

"Oh Tibbs... you are the same age as my father, and you are the only person on Earth who dares call me *Miss Hillman*. Can you not call me Mim like my father? It seems appropriate. I would so prefer that to just Hillman, which sounds so very... very stuffy... official, like staff... which I know that I am, of course... but..."

"Well, I must apologise Miss Hillman. I trust you know that I meant no disrespect?"

Mim laughed. "I doubt that 'disrespect' is even in your vocabulary Tibbs. Please... are we agreed? Just call me Mim... or Miriam if you must. It is not disrespectful to use the name my mother gave me."

"Of course... Miss Miriam. Now, what did you want to ask?"

"Hmm..." She took a deep breath and hardly knew how to start. "It is about my father. I told you that he had an accident at the warehouse and his foot was injured... it was bad. But even though his ankle is healing well enough, it just seems that he is not staying on top of things. It makes me think that the main problem is not his foot, but because he is alone with his thoughts

18

and his memories. The warehouse won't take him back because he is not mobile enough, but I thought it would be good if he could do something where being fast was not so important... where perhaps he could sit every so often but still work. Although he likes to read, he is not a book-work sort of person like yourself – he would not be able to do accounts. But something outside... something like gardening is more his style. He could weed the beds, or plant seedlings or water... anything like that. He is very good with plants, and I wondered if Mr Huang might need some help. I heard Marlie say that her vege' garden is not what it used to be... and I thought that would be perfect for Dad. He has been a hard worker all his life. Is there any way that you might consider this...please?" She blinked back tears.

Tibbs rubbed his temple and smiled. "You are a most caring daughter Miss Miriam. Your father must be so very proud of you."

"I hope so, but I think just now he is mostly sad. He needs something to get him out of the house. It is not good for him to be locked up with his thoughts..."

"You make a convincing case Miss Miriam. Look, I tell you what. I will go and call on him early next week and see if there is something that he is open to considering."

Mim smiled broadly with a deep sigh. "Oh, thank you Tibbs... Thank you so much!"

"Please Miss Miriam, can I ask something of you? Can you pray that I have the wisdom to know how to approach your father. People of our generation... we are strong and proud and not too inclined for charity."

"But a job is not charity... not when you get paid for what you do... right?"

"That is true... very true. It is all in the way we look at it."

* * *

Tibbs glanced around and checked his directions again. He tentatively knocked on the door. "Mr Hillman?" He paused and knocked again. Eventually he heard a rattle of the latch and the door opened.

Hillman stood there, scruffy and unkept, the stubble on his face was in that uncomfortable place between a shave and a beard. He looked warily at the intruder at his door. "So...?" was all he said.

"Did not Miss Hillman – your daughter, ah, Miss Miriam, did she not tell you that I would be coming?"

"What?" He screwed up his face as if the dim light of the dreary alleyway was hurting his eyes. "Oh yeah... you're the guy from the Big House."

"Yes, I am. Tiberius Barnes, at your service. Feel free to call me Tibbs. Grandfield... the 'Big House'... that is my job. But I came today to ask a favour of you... if I may explain?"

Mr Hillman looked suspiciously at the man's clean shoes and tidy coat. "Humph! Guess so... come in..."

He sat on the chair that Hillman pointed to with his crutch. Tibbs tried to look reassuring. "Mr Hillman, I want to congratulate you on your daughter. She is an exceptional young woman. She has obviously been raised well, and she is a delight."

Mr Hillman grunted again. "Of course. She's like her mother..."

"Is this your wife, Mr Hillman? She looks very happy," he said, indicating the framed portrait on the bench.

"Happy? We were... yes..." His eyes became moist, and he quickly took a drink of water from the grubby pottery tumbler by his side.

"Well, when I said I wanted to ask you a favour, I am a little embarrassed... as I don't quite know how to present it without being offensive. This is a little awkward for me."

"Huh. Awkward doesn't strike me as your style. Just spit it out."

"Well... okay." Tibbs took a breath and paused again before he began. "Grandfield – the said 'Big House' where I work, has an extensive garden... and we do have a very good gardener, a man named Mr Huang. However, to be frank Mr Hillman, Huang understands Mrs Whitaker... the lady of the house... very well. Her priority is the flower beds. Not just for the pleasant aspect of the grounds, but she is also partial to cut flowers in the drawing room, especially for her parties. Mr Huang's time is stretched just managing the grounds, and the flower beds. So, given the size of the horticultural task, I am looking for someone... who... well... I am looking for an extra pair of hands to focus on the vegetable side of things... herbs and such... watering and weeding and planting seedlings. But I am reluctant to advertise this in my usual circles because last time I had to filter through all sorts of people who were more interested in being seen at a big house, rather than working out the back, out of sight... when the job is so... unglamorous. So, when Miss Miriam..."

"Miriam? Did Mim put you up to this? She's been going on about me getting out."

"Well Miss Miriam did mention you were good with plants. I notice her work ethic, Mr Hillman, and that is a reference that I cannot ignore. And we don't need to tell her of our conversation if this would be more comfortable for you. But I have genuinely wondered if this might be something that you could help me with... at least a couple of days a week. Mrs Whitaker is very particular about the food served at her functions, and I am afraid that if things are left the way they are... then my Marlie's pantry garden will become neglected and that would..."

"Marlie? Marlie, of the basket with bread, and the vegetables, and those particularly lovely lemon tarts? This is *your* Marlie? She is your wife?"

"She is, Sir, yes. We have been married nigh twenty-five years. As you know, she has a generous heart, and I have been loathed to tell her that the vegetable garden is not a priority in favour of Mrs Whitaker's flowers."

"Marlie, huh. You know, fresh produce has been my life. I understand how important that is. How could she even do her job without her vege' garden?" he mused.

"I see that you understand me. Your discrete support in this matter would be a very big favour. I have a budget to manage of course, but there is enough for an assistant gardener if you would be inclined to help me in this..." He said it thoughtfully, as if calculating the surplus in his mind.

"But Mr Tibbs, surely Mim's told you of my accident at the warehouse, and the problem with my foot."

"So, it is not healing?" he frowned in concern. "Do you need a medical man?"

"Nah... it is healing well enough; I am sure of that... but it is just that I am slow at walking... and I have a crutch... at least for now."

"I have no issues with careful, Mr Hillman. I do prefer that to reckless young bucks running wild all over the place."

"Careful huh? Well, I would take real good care of the garden beds." He pointed to the volume on the table. My Mim has been bringing me books on gardening, 'cause she knows how I like that..."

Tibbs stared at the book and then looked away. "Well, that is a very thoughtful gesture, I am sure. So, is this something that you would be inclined to help me with Mr Hillman? Or do you need some time to consider it?"

"Nah... I reckon you can sign me on. I can be there tomorrow. You just let Mim know so she can come and help me get there."

"Miriam? You need her help?"

"Sure... she knows how it takes time... just to be careful, of course."

"Oh, I see. Well to avoid taking her away from her duties, perhaps tomorrow I can bring the Phaeton around to collect you. And then we can make a plan going forward. Does this agree with you Mr Hillman?"

"Guess so... now that I am a working man again." And he straightened himself as he stood to say goodbye, and he stood a little taller.

* * *

3

Mim moved from her favourite window-seat that overlooked the front garden, to a chair she had shifted to the other side of the nursery. That wide window looked over the vegetable garden out the back. The rising sun made long shadows over the garden beds. This was a time of day that Mim cherished... the calm before Miss Annabelle was awake and the day started. She watched her father's progress as he reconfigured the lay-out of the vegetable garden, so it was like a wheel, featuring Marlie's prize-winning lemon tree in the hub. Mim smiled as she saw him moving slowly around the beds of carrots, corn, and turnips. He took his shovel and started the process of digging up the potato patch.

"Ha-hu-hum Hillman, do you spend all your mornings gazing out the window?"

Mim quickly closed her women's journal and slid the book within its covers under her skirt. "Oh, good morning, Mr Meade. You are early this morning. Miss Anna is not even up yet. Your classes usually start after breakfast."

"They do, but as they say around here... a well-prepared tutor is a very effective tutor."

Mim chuckled. "Oh. I thought that only applied to the nursery staff! Although I am sure that Miss Anna is fast approaching the age when she will decide that she has outgrown a nursery-governess... and regardless of my preparedness, my role will be considered rather ineffective."

Mr Meade adjusted his spectacles, frowned and lowered his voice very seriously. "Do you think, Hillman, that they are considering letting you go? What would you do?"

"Oh Mr Meade, I have no concerns regarding my position really. Life at Grandfield requires that Mr and Mrs Whitaker have all the liberty to come and go without the restraints of a precocious eleven-year-old. My responsibilities might become less about dressing and amusement, but I will still be very much on duty."

"Oh, I see." He stared awkwardly at the books in his arm. "Ahh, Hillman, I was wanting to ask..." He cleared his throat and swallowed. "Miss Miriam, I want to ask if I could walk you to Church on Sunday. It is your day off."

Mim stared at him in surprise and then glanced down at the garden beds where her father was turning over the soil and knocking off sods from potatoes. He brushed off the dirt with his hands and rubbed each one with an old hessian bag before he added them carefully to the basket. There was nothing reckless about his slow and steady work. "Oh... umm..."

"Hillman, Miss Miriam... I would very much like to get to know you... outside of your nursery duties... if you know what I mean."

"Oh. I never considered that... um... walking to church... was something that you were... you know, thinking of." She glanced down at the magazine in her hand and felt as awkward as the loud silences between his swallows. Mr Meade started blinking furiously. Mim had always imagined the first time someone asked her to 'go walking' would cause her to feel excited and giggly, or nervous and blushing, or even just warm and friendly. But all that anticipation fizzled and disappeared, like the popping of Miss Anna blowing bubbles on a warm day. Her music teacher gave Anna bubbles as a breathing exercise. Mim learnt a lot from Anna's music teacher. Miss Lambert was an older lady who had a generous smile and a big bosom, with a long repertoire of ways to make fun out of boring exercises. But here, Mr Meade had done the opposite – he had taken something that should be fun and made it a chore.

"Well…" Mr Meade swallowed again. "Well, um… you like to read. You are always reading. I think it gives us common ground." He stood there shuffling his books, grimacing as if asking this was a responsibility akin to the duty required of walking a dog for exercise.

Mim raised her eyebrows and lifted the coloured journal so he could see the cover, the model's face was smiling, her cheeks painted with rouge, and her lips bright vermilion. He blushed and shuffled his feet.

"What I am reading is not exactly science, Mr Meade. I thought a tutor would expect something a little more intellectual than fashionable hats, and cooking recipes. It is your duty as an educator to expect more."

"Oh. You want more. Umm. Well… I… I think you are pretty. And I just wanted to ask…"

Now it was Mim's turn to swallow. He had no idea she was playing with him, and suddenly she was filled with guilt that she was the cat toying with a terrified mouse. She relented as he sighed and turned away. "Mr Meade, I would be honoured if you would accompany me to church on Sunday. I go to the early morning service."

He brightened up immediately, like a daisy opening to the morning sun that was now shining warmly though the window. "Oh! You do? This is very exciting. Very exciting indeed. It will be the best walk you will ever have going to church."

Mim smiled and nodded. "Well, that is… ambitious. I will be ready at half-seven."

"Yes. Yes! Very good Hillman. Very good."

He hummed a little tune as he settled himself at his desk, and tidied his books, and arranged his writing set a number of times to ensure it was positioned just so. He didn't even offer a glance in her direction again.

Mim sighed, as she smuggled her book back between the covers of the women's journal and retreated to get ready for the day. In truth, her first experience of being 'noticed' was a monumental disappointment. And she was annoyed that Mr Meade had intruded on those quiet morning hours before she needed to rouse Miss Anna and prepare her for breakfast.

* * *

Mim stared at the drizzling rain outside and tried not to think too much about the additional embarrassment of walking under an umbrella together with Mr Meade. Why had she not just said 'No'?

"Good morning, Miss Hillman. It is a beautiful day. I am delighted that we are walking together this morning." Mr Meade stood stiffly on the verandah outside the servant's entrance, his voice as dreary as the weather.

Mim nodded and offered some common pleasantries. This certainly was not her definition of delight.

"I have my umbrella. Did you not bring yours?" Mr Meade asked, staring at her arms that only held her bible wrapped in a shawl, to keep off the rain drops.

"Oh? You know, it *is* such a beautiful day, I had barely noticed that it was raining, allow me to run back and get my brolly." Mim ducked back inside, took a breath of absolute mortification, picked her umbrella off the stand, and then paused again to settle her breath and her dignity. When she stepped out again onto the back verandah, she had her smile plastered on, and her umbrella at the ready. Mr Meade stepped forward, as if he was zoning in for hug or a kiss, so Mim quickly put up her umbrella. He bounced back to avoid being poked in the eye. As they stepped out together, she was grateful their separate umbrellas made a very practical spacer and kept him at bay.

Mr Meade spoke formally about the pleasantness of raindrops, and the delight of the Sunday routine, and numerous other innocuous observations. In all truth, Mim had not the slightest idea on how to respond, so she mumbled more pleasantries and focused on keeping her hem and shoes out of the puddles. Just as they were nearing the church, the rain became heavier, and she was grateful she could legitimately hurry inside. During the service, when they stood to sing hymns, Mr Meade coyly glanced her way, then he'd fumble with his hymnal so he could bump her hand or brush her elbow, and each time they sat back down, he was far too close, so Mim would shuffle aside. By the end of Reverend Peters' sermon, she was jammed up against the end of the pew. When they finally stood to sing the doxology, Mim was convinced that Mr Meade was ready to propose. Once she was able to extract herself to the aisle, she quickly said her farewell, ducked her head and headed for the exit. She grabbed her umbrella and didn't worry about the rain but just ran and ran. Her breath was heavy as she turned into Thredpea Lane and bolted for her father's door.

She collapsed into a chair in the living room catching her breath. Her father emerged from his bedroom and stared bemused at Mim's wet hair that almost looked black in the shadows of the room. Like her mother's. Her Sunday dress was soaked. Without saying anything, he handed her a towel and went to make their morning cups of tea. She took his mug with a chuckle and a shake of her head.

"You seem to be in a good mood," he observed as he sat down heavily and propped his foot up on a chair. He would never say anything about his foot, but it ached. A lot. "Was Reverend Peters in good form?"

Mim shook her head again and sipped her tea.

Her father frowned. "You're looking like a drowned rat. You didn't have to come this morning... with the rain and all."

"Oh, it was a relief to come. Oh Dad, I think I have made a mistake," she said with a light laugh. The man was ridiculous. That part was amusing.

"I doubt getting caught in the rain qualifies as a serious error of judgement."

"Do you know Mr Meade, Miss Annabelle's tutor?"

"The stuffy, bookish one... with the eyeglasses?"

"Yep. Well, he asked to walk me to church this morning. I didn't really want to, but I felt sorry for him, so I said yes. I am sure he now thinks that means we are a couple... until death do us part. That was the mistake part."

"Huh. All that, just after a quick walk in the rain. Water might have melted his good sense. But a man with book-learning might be a good thing. At least that is different from the usual types around here."

"I seriously doubt 'good sense' applies. I should have said 'No', right from the start, but he was so uncomfortable and trying so hard. You know me... I felt sorry for him."

"He might become better company when he feels more relaxed. A pretty girl can be intimidating."

"Oh please. He said the 'rain is a delightful setting to go for a walk'. Perhaps, with the right company a walk in the rain might be romantic, but not with him."

"You know Mim, feeling sorry for a bloke is not enough to make something you can live with forever. Listen to your heart. Next time hold your ground. Every time you give in, you are reinforcing his version of things. Have mercy on the poor man and just put him out of his misery with the truth from the start. It is only fair."

"I know you are right. That is fatherly advice I will take." She took a sip of tea. "I like that you have settled in at Grandfield. I have a beautiful view of your garden from the window in the nursery. The way you are changing the whole layout is very creative."

"It's practical. The raised beds help my back. Got the idea from one of those books you brought me. I'm planting the same types of veggies in the various sections together... beets and turnips, leeks and onions... tomatoes and capsicum... Brussels-sprouts, cauliflower and broccoli. And I have a whole section for Marlie's herbs... oregano, sage, parsley... chives. These fancy Whitaker's like their herbs."

"Well, I think the stone walls along the path create a wonderful classic feel. Just like everything you do, it doesn't just look good, it is also functional."

"The layout is helping track the crop rotations better. And I like the idea that you can look out your window over a garden that doesn't look like a graveyard. It will take a couple of cycles to finish it, and when I told Mr Tibbs these plans are more in keeping with a grand old House, he seemed happy enough."

"Well, I know Marlie is excited. This garden will provide all the produce she needs. I remember our vege patch at our other house; it was always giving us something to eat."

"Mrs Marlie is a lovely soul. She gave me a list of vegetables she wants, and she saves all her seeds. I have planned out the year, so soon we should have a steady supply of seasonal produce."

"Oh Dad, I am so happy this is working."

"I've taken Tibbs up on his offer of a room in the quarters during the week. With my foot as it is, it is too much, toing and froing. But it is good to come back on the weekend. It feels like a rest."

"Yeah, I agree. It is nice to have our own space that isn't Grandfield."

* * *

Mr Whitaker stared at Tibbs with a severe frown. "You say that you knew about the books going missing?"

"Sir, I am saying they were borrowed. Not missing and certainly not stolen."

"Borrowed? That's an extraordinarily presumption to make about this situation. There is a lot of money tied up in this Library Tibbs."

"I well understand Sir. However, I believe it is worth noting that the library has only been accessed to serve the wellbeing of its occupants or to make a contribution to Grandfield estate."

"What do you mean? I could legitimately sack you and every one of the culprits," Mr Whitaker said with a deep frown. "It is offensive to think these books were taken by staff."

"Borrowed, Sir. *Borrowed* by the staff."

He grunted again. "Offensive none the less." He took a book from the shelf and caressed it affectionately like a beloved pet. Tibbs had never seen him show any attachment to his library prior to this idea that it was being intruded upon by less worthy readers.

"But the knowledge acquired Sir, has already shown beneficial results. The gardener has been reading about horticulture on larger estates. Miss Annabelle's governess has an improved knowledge and can answer questions that Miss Annabelle's enquiring mind demands. She helps Miss Annabelle with her homework, set by Mr Meade...".

Mr Whitaker glanced up from the book, confused. "Who?"

"Miss Annabelle's tutor, Sir: Mr Meade. Even Marlie has been studying herbs for your dishes. These are all matters that are related to the smooth functioning of Grandfield estate."

Mr Whitaker stared at Tibbs with a curl of his lip. His eyes held a suspicious glint. "I'm calling your bluff. I don't believe you for a second. They are just being presumptuous and crossing a line. Go get that gardener. I am going to test your account of this. And if it doesn't pass to my satisfaction, they will all get the sack. Make sure that gardener brings back the book he has taken."

Tibbs straightened his collar and smoothed his brow. "Yes Sir," he said quietly. Mr Whitaker was usually a reasonable man. Tibbs turned smartly on his heel and went to the gardeners' outbuilding where he found Hillman sorting through the dried seeds at the bench. "Mr Hillman, I will not lie. Mr Whitaker is very upset. I urge you to think of the most creative justification as to why you read these books. He is upset enough to terminate our agreement."

Hillman looked at Tibbs as he took off his gardening boots and changed into his house-shoes. He saw anxiety leaking through Tibbs' impeccable calm. Perhaps it was the flush on his cheekbones. "Hmm. Serious, huh," was all that he said.

"Very serious," Tibbs said under his breath, as he quietly prayed all the way to the library. He felt like an executioner taking an inmate for his last walk.

"Mr Whitaker, Sir, this is Hillman, the gardener."

"Isn't our Gardener Chinese?"

"Mr Huang does not read English Sir. The book issue doesn't impact him, Sir."

Mr Whitaker stared severely at Mr Hillman. "So, you have been stealing my books," he said.

Hillman calmly took in his employer's agitation. He seemed like a man who needed to know he was important, and required reassurance that his territory was not being invaded by barbarians. "Well Sir, I would more likely call it research."

"Research! What could you possibly want to research that a gardener doesn't normally know? Isn't plants your job?"

Hillman looked down at his hands. His fingernails were rough and dirty. "Well Sir, I could show you. I brought the book. But normally I would not dare open the pages, when my hands are not washed."

"No matter. Tibbs can do it."

Hillman nodded and passed him the book. "There's a plate in the centre, there abouts. Show him that." It was the inspiration for his circular layout of the vegetable garden. That would be evidence enough that his reading was research.

Tibbs turned to the page, lifted his brow and turned the book around. Mr Whitaker stared at it. "This? This is what you have been researching?" He took the book from Tibbs and walked over to the window and stared out over the grounds.

"Yes Mister. I am very aware that these grand estates require a little more than just the usual garden beds. They require something with style... that feels more... proper. It is not just about cultivating... it is growing plants with... the right sort of feel. I could not plan these types of things, without the books because it is not what I'm used to. The books help me think about what would be more fitting for Grandfield Park, Sir."

Mr Whitaker curled his lip thoughtfully. "Hmm. Fitting. I agree. And where would we put this glasshouse?"

"Glasshouse, Sir?"

"Yes..." Mr Whitaker turned the book around, and Hillman stared at a plate of a grand, ornate glass solarium, large and wide, filled with ferns and exotic orchids. "My wife would appreciate something like this. She likes flowers."

"Oh... a glasshouse? Of course. Glasshouse. Ahh... I am... I am more used to calling them common greenhouses Sir, but 'Glasshouse' is right. I am sure a Glasshouse has the right feel. You were asking... what exactly...?"

"Where would we put it? If you are researching this, you would have obviously thought about that."

"Yes. Well... I was thinking... it needs to be out to the side... over towards the tennis court. A feature like this should not be out the back with the vegetables. It needs to be seen by Mrs Whitaker's visitors, so they can appreciate some of the unusual flowers we can grow there." Hillman cleared his throat and stared at his feet and noticed a hole in his sock visible above the line of his house shoes. He should remind Mim to mend that for him.

When they were dismissed, Tibbs had never been so grateful to reprimand his staff. It was made clear that the books were not to go off the estate. Mim could only go into the library after her workday, when she was absolutely certain that Mr and Mrs Whitaker were out visiting or had retired. Tibbs even congratulated Hillman on his Glasshouse initiative.

Hillman nodded quietly and said, "Kinda relieved that I can't give directions to save my life. My Missus was always sayin' that. Only this time, being vague landed you at the glasshouse page and probably saved my life... or at least our jobs. Pretty sure a vege-patch would not have cut it." And he went back to his garden beds and dug around the radishes, and thought about flash gentry glasshouses, and how building the flashiest sort of solarium was to become his next project.

* * *

4

Mim checked the corridor again and skirted through the shadows. She jolted as she passed some figurines dressed as English Christmas Carollers, who stood in their top-hats and bonnets, holding their sheet music like apparitions from Christmas-Past out of the Dicken's novel. Mrs Whitaker ramped up the festivities to another level of feverish entertainment to be ready to host her annual Christmas Gala as soon as December opened its doors. It seemed too early for the entire house to look like Christmas had exploded all over it. This evening was Mim's weekly excursion into the restricted realm of the library. She had her father's book, and a couple of her own, in a simple cloth bag tucked under the arm. The lamp she held in her hand was turned down low. Silence creaked through the house as she opened the door to the library. Even this room was decorated with traditional boughs of holly. She wondered why they would bother when hardly anyone came here, and Mr Whitaker wasn't a fan of the Christmas season anyway.

Mim could smell the smoke of Mr Whitaker's cigars as she closed the door behind her. This room was shut up most of the time, so that smell never went away. And then she saw a stub of a cigar smouldering in the pedestal ashtray, the glow of its halo fading as it sat in the dark. Her mother had told stories of curtains blowing onto unattended ashtrays or them being knocked over and causing a fire. She went over and quickly stubbed it out, and then turned to carefully place her lamp on a wall bracket while she returned the borrowed books. She deliberately wiped the bound covers with her apron and made sure the alignment of the books along the edge of the shelf were exactly even. She certainly did not want Tibbs calling her in again because she had been sloppy. She went to the other side of the library to select something for her father. The heritage of this house was a family of avid gardeners – a trait that seemed to have skipped this generation of Whitakers entirely. Still, it meant there were plenty of books to choose from. Overseeing the surprise Glasshouse project made Mim smile, and she hummed a little tune. If there was ever an accidental gardener, it was her father. But he was persistent and determined enough to make a success of whatever he turned his hand to. Her mother would say that of him – that he was a man who would keep trying until he turned mud into porcelain. She smiled as she thought of her father's comment about being a rock weathered into mud, and wondered if her mother's observation would be a metaphor of the next phase of his live... crafting high-end beautiful porcelain. Mim selected a book on garden structures and flicked through the pages under the lamplight to make sure there was a section on glasshouses.

After Mim tucked that book into her bag, she turned up the lamp, adjusted the ladder, climbed a few runs, and still humming, ran her hand along the bookshelves anticipating what her next adventure might be. She would only choose two volumes for herself, so she wanted to make sure her choices were... 'discerning'. That's why she took her time: once these books went to her room, she would feel obliged to read to the very last page. Mim held an unspoken loyalty to her authors, and the editors, and the printers, and the binders... all the people who had gone to so much trouble to make this book available for her. It was a token of respect that she would read it front cover to back cover. An unfinished book felt like an uneaten meal or a discarded glass of drink. Wasteful. But perhaps that was another privilege of the rich and advantaged. She climbed down the ladder and placed her book options on the desk to finalise her choices. There was an unfinished glass of port sitting beside a classic bust of some Roman Caesar who presided over the desk like he was considering which empire he would conquer next. Mim had named this Roman icon "Maximillian" which meant *"The Greatest"*, a name that suited him as he stared arrogantly with his marble gaze over a free-standing globe of the world. Perhaps this great Caesar was using the left-over port to toast victory over his conquered realms. Ironic. Still, it was wasteful to leave a glass unfinished. Why not pour less? More evidence that the Whitakers were careless and did not take responsibility seriously. No wonder Anna was like she was. Mim hesitated. Perhaps the dutiful thing would be to return the drinking-glass to the scullery and wash it up, so that the collection of crystal would sit there sparkling in the morning next time they came to the library. She picked up the glass to move it to the side, so that at least she would not accidently knock it off the edge.

Suddenly a severe voice spoke, breaking the silence. "You've killed my cigar, but you are not stealing my port!" Mim jumped, squealed, the glass dropped from her fingers, hit the side of the desk and crystal shattered into a million pieces. The dark tawny liquid splattered over her books, across the desk and dribbled onto the rug under the globe stand. A young man... not Mr Whitaker, emerged from the shadows of a deep leather winged reading chair and stood to his feet. His thick hair was slicked across in a severe part, and his brocade smoking jacket looked like a Japanese kimono as it fell to the top of his house slippers. The quilted collar matched the turned-up cuffs on the sleeves, wide and pretentious.

Mim grabbed her books, dabbing the liquid off their covers with her apron as she backed up. "I am so sorry Sir. I didn't know any visitors had come in here. I will be going."

"Hmm. You know you cannot just leave. You are obliged to clean up your mess: the mess that you made with *my* drink."

"I thought it had been left by Mr Whitaker. I am sorry Sir. You startled me. I had no idea you were sitting here all along. I will get some cloths and attend to that immediately."

"Glad to hear it," he said, stepping around the fragments of glass, some of them crunching under his step. He flicked a latch on the globe and the top of the world flipped open to reveal a drinks bar with glasses lined up inside. The man casually poured himself another drink, retrieved his cigar from the ashtray, sat down to relight it. He glanced up at her as she stood there staring at him in the shadows. "Are you not getting some cloths? To clean up your mess?"

"Oh yes Sir. Going. Now." She put her books on a chair and paused at the door. "Sir, will you be here when I get back?"

"I have no reason to leave. You interrupted me... not the other way 'round."

"What I mean is... do you want me to wait until you leave, before I return."

"I think that carpet is screaming to be restored to its pristine Persian state. Due haste is appropriate I would say. Port can stain."

"Yes, yes of course." Mim blushed brightly and disappeared. She returned with two buckets – one filled with water, an empty one to deposit the broken glass, some cooking soda, a swag of cleaning rags and a brush. The man had lit the other lamps around the room, muted only by the haze generated by his cigar.

Mim glanced across at him as she started to pick up the larger fragments of glass. He emphatically puffed his cigar, blowing smoke rings as he sat with his legs crossed in the big brown leather chair. She moved items off the desk, carefully wiping them over with the cleaning rag. She brushed the fragments from the desk and carpet and deposited them in the empty bucket. The man silently watched her while he continued to puff on his cigar. Mim paused... but did not look at him. "You know, I would be far more comfortable if you would not stare. Surely you can read a book or something."

"I'm good. Thanks."

Mim stood up, and carefully wiped down the desk, her lips pressed in concentration so not to scratch the polished surface with any remaining fine fragments of glass that might be unseen. "No disrespect Sir, but surely as a visitor of Grandfield Park, you could find another, more pleasant place, to smoke your cigar... if you have no interest in books."

"I doubt it. It is late, so I don't want to disturb the others, and I'm not going outside. I am perfectly content here."

Mim grunted. "Perfectly inconvenient..." she muttered, as she arranged the items back on the desk as precisely as they were before. Caesar again stood staring over his realms.

"I'm surprised to find you here. It does not seem like the usual pattern of Grandfield to allow servants to borrow books from their esteemed library."

That he would call her a 'servant' instead of 'staff' was a bit archaic. "Well, at least you do not accuse me of stealing."

"No, you pay too much attention to return your books with care and precision, to allow me to accuse you of that."

"Just so you know, Tibbs covered it with Mr Whitaker, so whether you approve or not, I have permission to be here. But my access also carried the proviso that no one would be around while I make my weekly selection."

"Oh. Hence why you are so keen to evict me."

Mim got down on the floor and swept the glass into a heap, smearing spilt port everywhere as she did. How could one small portion of port-wine spread so far? She crawled into the space under the desk, and then emerged again. "How was I to know anyone would be sitting here, smoking and drinking port in the dark? Even a candle would have given me a clue that you did not want to be interrupted."

"Darkness and quietness are not unpleasant... more welcoming than your incessant chatter."

"Then I will be quiet." She moved across and started on the port-wine stain that had bled into the carpet. She sprinkled the cooking soda on the stains and then rubbed it into a paste. She muttered to herself as she wiped it up, rinsed her cloth in the bucket of water and repeated the process. Over and over, each splatter was given the same attention. "How long are you visiting here at Grandfield?" she asked frankly as she inspected the carpet with a lamp turned up high. She found another spot that was missed and got back down on her knees, giving that the soda treatment as well.

"I thought you were going to be quiet. It seems that you are quite incapable of doing that. You are a chatterbox that cannot close the lid."

"Well sure, that is a common enough observation regarding my nature, but it may be to your benefit if you answer my question. For if I know how long you are here, I will duly avoid the library for the duration of your visit." She stood up and lifted the lamp inspecting the carpet carefully.

"Just until after Christmas. I don't stay for New Year's."

"But that is weeks away! Will you be here all this time?"

"Yes... and then I will leave," he said with an amused smirk. "But you don't have to cancel your library visits while I'm here. That would not be fair."

Mim dared to look at him then. Yes, he was much younger than Mr and Mrs Whitaker, and yet he didn't look or feel out of place. In fact, he seemed very much at home... and his eyes were laughing at her in the lamp light. "Oh. Well... welcome to Grandfield Park Sir. I trust you enjoy your visit." Mim frowned, slung the strap of her bag of books over her shoulder, picked up her buckets and rags and promptly left the library, closing the door behind her.

* * *

5

"Oh, it is terrible! I hate Christmas!" Anna stomped her foot and refused to add another ornament to the Christmas tree they were decorating.

Mim stood quietly looking at Anna's red, angry face. "You do? But the house looks so pretty with all its decorations. I want the nursery to look just as cheerful as the rest of the house for you." It was the only room that had not been drowned with all things festive, and that was because Mim had specifically asked to decorate the nursery as a creative activity with Anna. The plan was to distract her from the Gala.

But Anna wasn't having a bar of it. "Sure. It can be just like everything else around here. It will be all decorated up, with fancy balls and bows, but underneath there is nothing that is good or kind. I wish I lived in a plain old house, with plain old people, with plain old food and then no one would ever want to visit."

"Anna, I know you are disturbed by all the visitors. Tonight is the Christmas Gala, and perhaps you are worried that you are missing out."

"I *am* missing out! It is not fair. I am not allowed to go anywhere or do anything, or touch anything. I am locked up here like a prisoner, and you are my warden. It has been horrible since Max has come."

"Max? Your brother has arrived home to visit?" Of course. Grandfield's son was a favourite with the staff; the house was abuzz with the notion that the famous heir was home again, just as he did every year, to attend the Gala.

"Yes! You are absolutely right: he is just a visitor. Grandfield is not really his home – because he is never here. So now I officially disown him: he is not my brother at all. It was like this last year as well. Mother just goes on and on about Max! Max this, Max that. Max her first born. Max her son. Max her heir. Max her favourite. I hate him!"

"Perhaps... since he is your brother, you could be a little patient?" How Mim wished her own brother was still around so she could be annoyed and impatient with him all over again. "Come Anna, he can't be that bad, he is your family after all." Mim didn't feel very convincing in delivering that statement, after all, her family were Whitakers, but she came alongside Anna and tried to soothe her bothered dramatics anyway.

But the girl stomped uncontrollably. "Oh, but he is! He is an ugly, vicious troll from the worst imagination story you have ever read!"

"Oh, I am, am I? Really? I am an ugly, vicious Troll!"

Mim spun around and gasped. Her face paled as she came face to face with the man from the library, standing casually by the door. He was dressed in a dinner suit, his bowtie was impeccably tied, his smart polished shoes reflecting the lights of the room across the toecap. "*This* is your brother? *You* are Maxwell Whitaker?" Absent Max, the illusive heir of Grandfield, the crown prince, the handsome celebrity whose fame... or infamy, was whispered through corridors and halls of Grandfield all year round.

Anna was instantly transformed. "Oh, my Troll! You are here!" And she jumped up into his arms with a laugh! "You took your time," she whispered in his ear, affectionately ruffling her fingers through his hair.

He ducked his head. "Mind the locks, Gruffling. I have to present myself to the masses later. Got to look respectable." Mim stared confused as he spun Anna around with a chuckle. "How *is* my littlest Billy-Goat-Gruff? Are you still my little Gruffling, even after your huffing and puffing about all my worst faults?"

"Always. And I am so much better now you are here."

"Well Gruffling," he said with a handsome smile, "it is a shame I am so ugly and vicious because it means this Troll will just have to take his gift elsewhere." He set her down and pulled a wrapped gift from inside his jacket.

Anna grabbed it with both hands and started to rip off the paper. "You are just like Mother, trying to buy me with gifts," she laughed. "It might be working, so I had better open it and see." She turned it over. It was a brand-new edition of the Dicken's novel, '*A Christmas Carol.*' "Oh. That looks drab," she said with a disappointed frown. "Well, never mind…" and she tossed it aside.

Mim was mortified. "Anna! That is terribly rude! Apologise this instant! You must say thank you for your gift. Anna, that present was a thoughtful gesture. You need to think about your manners whether you are excited by a gift or not."

"Oh okay. I'm sorry. I am sorry Max that you are a Troll who cannot give exciting gifts. Besides, when I *do* think about it, it *really* is not a great gift… at least not for me." Anna laughed and looked very amused.

Max didn't seem offended that his gift was rejected and so quickly discarded. He picked it up off the chair and waved it in front of Mim. "Perhaps your governess would prefer to read it?" Mim's eyes hungrily followed the book as he waved it about. "Because recently, I heard it suggested that reading might be more interesting than sitting alone in the dark, smoking cigars and sipping port. That's what governesses do, right… read when no one is watching?"

"Huh. I doubt it," said Anna with a shrug. "Hillman only ever reads stupid magazines."

"Does she really?" he asked with a curious raise of his brow. "Well, I will write an inscription that says this book is now the property of Hillman, the Grandfield governess. She might be able to expand her horizons to include some more classic reading."

"You can't do that," Mim stammered. "That book is a perfectly respectable gift for your sister. It is beautiful, in fact."

"Well, it seems she does not think so," he said with an offhand shrug. He went over to the tutor's desk, swiped the hair from his eyes and picked up a pen and scribed on the inside cover: *The property of Miss Miriam Hillman. From Max Whitaker. 1909.'* Max blew on the ink until it was dry and then closed the cover and pressed it firmly into her hands. "I think you will appreciate it more than any spoilt eleven-year-old."

Anna pulled at her brother with a twinkle, "Since I am so spoilt, and your present was such a monumental failure, you will have to give me something else instead," she said.

"This Troll demands that you name your price... or I will chop you up into a thousand miniscule pieces and eat you for dinner!"

Anna jumped up on a chair and stood regally, lifting her arm high as a royal sceptre. "I decree that the Troll will not go to the stupid Christmas Gala, and he will stay here with me instead... all night!"

He screwed up his nose in disappointment. "Sorry Gruffling, I have to show up. You know that I do."

"Why? Who is going to miss you?"

"How about I sneak out after dessert? In the meantime, I have another idea..."

"Really?"

"Yes... but you will have to finish decorating the Christmas tree... and...". There was a knock at the Nursery door. "I wonder..." Max said mysteriously as he raised his brows curiously and opened the door wide with a flourish. He ushered in Tibbs and his daughter, Chrissy, pushing a trolley loaded with Christmas treats. "Happy Christmas-Gala Night Anna!"

"Chrissy! You are here! Can you stay?"

Chrissy bounced around in a dance. "Yes! We are having our own Gala! Your brother arranged it."

"A real Chrissy party!" Anna declared with excitement, and the girls laughed hysterically at her funny pun.

Mim handed each of them some brightly coloured baubles, while Max and Tibbs quietly retreated, and the girls debated how to decorate the prettiest tree in all the land. They romped and danced to Christmas carols that Anna demanded Mim sing. They arranged a rug under the tree, and laid there staring up through its branches, giggling and looking at their ornaments from a completely new angle. Then they speculated on what they wanted for Chrissy-presents; and what they were going to do over the Chrissy holidays; and which guest wore the wildest Chrissy hat from the myriad of visitors who had invaded Grandfield for the celebrations. Mim arranged Marlie's Chrissy treats on a tray near the tree – shortbread, and apple tartlets, and fruit-mince pies, and gingerbread biscuits, and a deliciously moist Chrissy cake with cherries, accompanied by Marlie's lemon cordial... and the girls feasted on their Chrissy picnic under the Chrissy tree with unembarrassed delight. They giggled and laughed their way through the evening until Mim dimmed the lamps, brought cushions and rugs for them to lie on under the tree, and lit just a couple of flickering candles in the room. Mim quietly sang a couple of soothing carols and the girls whispered and smothered their giggles late into the night until they collapsed into slumber and their next story was overwhelmed by the regular breathing of sleep. Mim quietly covered them both with a light blanket, and nodded as she admired their contented faces still smiling in their sleep.

The Nursery door opened, and Max stepped quietly over to the tree and quietly gazed on the two fresh faces still embracing each other in their sleep. He took off his jacket and tossed it on a chair. Then he came over to Mim, who was propped up on cushions in the window seat, reading in the lamplight of a single lantern sitting on the sill. Mim moved her legs aside as he sat down; he casually loosened his bowtie and kicked off his shoes. He sat there fiddling with his cufflinks, that glinted in the lamplight. Mim stared at them mesmerised. Mother-of-pearl, chequered with onyx and blue lapis stone, studded with diamonds around the rim. Too pretty for a man, but ostentatious enough to suit Max Whitaker. "Miss Miriam, I am sorry I could not extract myself earlier. But I did promise Anna I would come back, so when my sister grills you in the morning, you can bear witness to the fact that I was indeed faithful to my word. Did they have a good night?"

His question drew her attention back to his face, his eyes. Pupils, black like onyx, blue lapis iris, mother-of-pearl white... a careless delight for life that glinted like diamonds. She swallowed and answered his question.

"The best. They are so blessed to be such good friends. I hardly know of another friendship that clicks so perfectly. They have only just stopped giggling and laughing... and I think from the smiles still on their faces, some of their jokes continue in their dreams."

Max eyes glinted with a smile. "I'm glad. I envy their age when everything is all in, nothing is held back, social expectations mean nothing, and they can enjoy moments with such wholehearted devotion."

"It was a kind of you to arrange this."

"You sound completely surprised. I can do kind."

"In truth, I am surprised you would support your sister cavorting with the staff help."

"You should not listen to every report you hear about me. I am not the troll that even Anna would accuse me of being."

"Sir, I am having a hard time reconciling all the reports I hear about you, with what I have seen. There are some big discrepancies between the indifferent absent sibling... the rumours of the handsome philanderer... the gruff cigar waving man in his pretentious smoker's jacket... Anna's ugly, vicious Troll... even the slick heir in his stylish dinner suit... with the *kind* older brother who celebrates a children's folktale and captures memorable moments with a best-friend, regardless of status, to create a catalogue of childhood experiences for his sister. This is more bizarre than, as Anna would say, "the worst imagination story you could ever read". Can all this really be the same person?"

"They may not be. I highly recommend that you investigate further... just to be sure."

"You are an enigma Mr Whitaker. I do not know what to think."

"Well at least you think I am handsome."

"I did not say you were... only that it was rumoured."

He shrugged carelessly. "True, you did. So, did you like your gift?"

"Anna's present?"

"*Your* gift. I gave it to you."

"Ahhh..." Something dawned on her then, and she swallowed hard. "You planned this. And Anna was in on the joke! That girl should act on a stage. You wanted me to be upset that she rejected your gift. It was an amusing stunt. I trust you were entertained at my expense."

"True, true, true, and true. All true. But you didn't answer the question: do you like the book? Was it worth the conspiring effort?"

She opened the magazine in her lap, to reveal a book held between its pages. She was reading *A Christmas Carol.* "It is magnificent storytelling, with a poignant message. Of course I love it. I think the only legitimate excuse one could offer for not being able to appreciate the quality of such a gift would be that you are eleven years old. She may appreciate it when she is older."

Max raised his brow and stared at the magazine in her lap. "So, this is why my sister thinks you are a shallow, inattentive reader of common gossip and trash. This is your book. I gave it to you. You don't have to hide it within the covers of a magazine."

"Oh." She blushed and pushed the magazine aside. "Habit, I guess. You see, I have noticed that some people are disturbed when the hired-help... '*servants*' was your own turn of phrase... presume to read books that are not in keeping with expectations associated with their particular station. Your sister is one of them."

"That is only because she has never had those expectations challenged. You reinforce them with your charade."

"I am protecting my job."

"Then get another job! You don't have to work here at Grandfield and be stuffed into a small box that is completely outdated."

"I am amused that you think Grandfield is small, and I wonder how the acclaimed heir of its hallowed halls is so determined to call it outdated.

"I think you can do better."

"Of course I can get a different job. But this house is within commuting distance to my father's home, and now that he has a job here as the secondary gardener it is providential that my job is here too. It is important that I am close to him."

"Providential hey? Well Miss Miriam Hillman, who is the enigma now?"

"That is not at all puzzling. I need to work. This location suits my circumstances. My father has an opportunity that he is fortunate to secure. That is all that matters for now."

***

Part 2

The Chapters of Life: Grandfield Hospital

1916

6

Mim paused at the large stone gateway and read the sign erected there. *'Grandfield Hospital – Military Rehabilitation Facility.'* She pressed her lips and sighed as her eyes ran over another line at the bottom of the sign – *"For the welfare of Soldiers who served in the Great War."* This war was not great, and it was still going on... and yet that is how people referred to it, in the newspapers, in conversation. *"The war that named itself,"* they said. Today, she wasn't coming to visit her father at work in the garden; today she was coming to work – full-stop. And that made today very different.

When she had walked out of Grandfield, no longer Miss Annabelle's governess, she finally felt herself swimming free from the riptide. A little tired, a little weak, but confident that life had broader possibilities. She hadn't been pulled beneath the undertow and she hadn't drowned. There was something about that conversation with Max Whitaker that had stimulated possibilities in her. Most people expected that since she was a governess, that her Grandfield position would logically be the stepping stone to teaching. But her encounter with Mr Meade, did nothing to inspire her to teach frustrated eleven-year-olds for the rest of her working life. What she did want to do, was to help people like her dad get back on their feet. Nursing was her definition of the 'better' that Max had alluded to.

So Mim applied to a number of hospitals and signed away her freedom with the first acceptance letter she received. She couldn't leave Grandfield quick enough. After her training had been completed, she worked on various wards, but she never really settled on that 'one' type of nursing that suited her best. Her father's foot injury inclined her toward orthopaedics. She was considering more training in this area when war had been declared.

Mim hadn't counted on a war, or the squealing pressure that put the whole world on edge, like a kettle about to boil dry. When her dad had intimated that they were going to seconder Grandfield Park as a hospital in support of the war effort, Mim set aside enlisting for military service overseas. This was to be a facility for rehabilitating returned servicemen and veterans. This was her opportunity to serve on the home front.

The changes to Grandfield were a constant topic of conversation. Mr and Mrs Whitaker moved into the Stablemaster's Lodge. They were keeping on many of the house-staff to support the hospital. Tibbs still managed the running of the property. Marlie still cooked in the kitchen. Macy Hargrave, the seamstress, now made nurses uniforms, attended to mending patient's clothes, pyjamas, and linen. Not quite the same style of fashionable sewing she was used to. Mim's dad not only kept his job, but his duties had expanded to supply the kitchen with produce that would cater for all staff and patients. Mr Huang had long gone. Flowerbeds were no longer required, and her father had several groundsmen working with him to keep up the demand for food. Mr Hillman lived and breathed his garden. The Glasshouse was stripped of its exotic plants and became the nursery of seedlings for the additional vegetable garden beds he had installed. Her father had been so hopeful that Mim would transfer back to work at Grandfield again. He mentioned it every time she visited, gently urging her that this would give them more time together in a world frantic with war. One thing this war did, was to reinforce the value of family. Everywhere they looked, families were being sacrificed and ripped apart. Mim acutely felt the privilege of being with her dad, joining hands, and working for a common cause as a family.

So Mim carried her suitcase up the driveway, and moved back into the Grandfield Servant's Quarters, or as the section was now known – the Nurses Quarters. The nursing staff were under the supervision of Sister Ellie Pollard, who was answerable to the Matron of the main hospital in the region. It was all very strange and although the house facade had the same grand lines, nothing on the inside of the building was familiar anymore. The Grandfield she once knew, was no longer recognisable.

* * *

"Quickly Sister! This way. I need your help."

Mim put down the chart she was writing and promptly followed Doctor Redmond down the corridor. There had been a large number of admissions this morning. There was a lot to do. The doctor passed the bedrooms that were now fitted out as wards. They stopped at Room Seven. Doctor Redmond closed the door behind them. Whereas most of the other rooms had six bunks lining the walls, only a single hospital bed stood in the middle of this large room. There was a fireplace and a window looking over the courtyard covered with heavy curtains. A bare desk, a chair and a screen gave the room a stark, sterile feel. Mim looked at the bandages around the soldier's head. "I thought we were only getting rehabilitation admissions. This doesn't exactly look like rehab."

"Well noted Sister. This man was repatriated as a 'cot case' – requires constant medical care. His injuries: mustard gas burns mostly; some shrapnel abrasions. Compound, complicated fractures of the tibia and fibula – left leg. They have already been set by the surgeon. But the injury to his eyes and throat means he is unfit for service, so he won't be going back."

"Is he going to live? His whole body is covered in bandages!"

57

"Your observation skills are not letting you down. But you should know that this patient is here on a special directive from the Brigadier. We are not told who he is... for security reasons I suppose... but when we get this sort of notification from the Army then one can assume this is a person of significance. Another directive – he is to have his own private nurse allocated. You are going to be that person."

"Me?" asked Mim with her eyes wide.

"Yes. You have done your full training. Most of the staff here have only done abridged courses. This person is to be given the best of what we have. I obviously can't pull Sister Pollard off due to her supervisory responsibilities... so you are it."

"Sir, if I am the best... then you have a real problem. I don't have the experience required to intensively nurse a patient like this."

The Doctor almost laughed. "Sister, I don't have time to argue. I really don't. I only have time to make sure that this man is cared for with what we have available. You are to report only to me, and you must not discuss his situation with anyone. Consider this notice of your reassigned duties."

"Okay... so – I am assigned to his care. Confidential issues noted. Who else will be working with me?"

"What do you mean?"

"I mean... which other nurse will be working this case, to rotate shifts?"

Dr Redmond wobbled his head as if considering something. "Hmm. I suppose that is a reasonable question, but unfortunately, I don't have a reasonable answer. I can't spare anyone else. There is a war on. The bunk behind that screen is for your use. Your meals will be taken in here. This room was chosen because it has an adjoining bathroom. You have exclusive use of it... mostly.”

“Mostly?”

“Well, you know... these old houses. They are working on upgrading more appropriate plumbing for a hospital, so bathrooms are limited. I say that to remind you to keep the doors locked from the inside. Here is the key which is to be kept on your person at all times. The idea is not to keep you in, but to keep others out. The burns, and the sensitive nature of the situation requires that the patient be nursed in isolation. I trust you appreciate the difference.”

“Doctor, let me get this straight: I am under ward arrest, on twenty-four-hour care, looking after a man who doesn’t even have a name?”

“‘Ward arrest’ is a little... no... you are probably right: *ward arrest* is a fair description. Obviously, he does have a name – we are just not privy to it.”

“Then what do I call him?”

“Anything you like, I suppose. His chart has been given to us as Case File 7285.”

“Are you sure he is someone important? Perhaps he is going to be court marshalled... perhaps he is a war-criminal, kept here to go to trial?”

“Well, I seriously doubt they would give a criminal this kind of attention. Letting them die is its own form of justice when resources are so stretched. I acknowledge the situation is certainly unusual. Normally acute patients like this are managed in the larger hospitals, or the clinics overseas. However, they must have their reasons for getting him back here, given the flood of repatriation cases on the way. But whatever their reasons, the army considers him important. I think it would be safe to assume that he holds some sort of rank. Even if he does not, and it is as you suppose, this man poses little threat, because presently, he is heavily sedated. Keep him alive. Help him get better. There is a specific request to chart any ramblings or statements he makes... even if they don't seem relevant to you. They have told me they will drop in frequently to check his status. If you need anything urgent outside my usual rounds – use the staff bell on that cord. Have a list ready of any supplies that need replenishing; linen and your uniforms will be refreshed daily or as you require. Spares and supplies are in that wardrobe. Meals for you and your patient will be provided through the hatch. I will circulate the idea that this patient is highly contagious, and you are both in mandated isolation."

Mim stared at the doctor with wide eyes. "Sir, I have to say, this feels like I am being punished for a crime I didn't commit."

"Sister, I have to say... this entire war is punishing us for a fight we didn't start. Your country thanks you for your service."

* * *

Mim sat in the shadows and stared at the bed. She had taken the patient's observations and filled out his chart. His face was rough with beard, and his delirious restlessness was soundless. She held a cup and mitred out the fluids through his gastric-tube. She checked his wound dressings and reviewed all the prescribed care that had been laid out in his chart.

One minute she was on a hectic ward filling out admissions, and the next moment she is locked inside a room, for an unknown period of time. Mim found the silence oppressive, even with all the work needed to look after him. Nurses had various versions of rules and theories about talking with patients. Some nursing-sisters absolutely would not chat with their patients: their work was to be kept professional, and as far as Mim could tell, 'professional' meant cold and aloof. Others said it was good for the staff and the patients to see the human side of each other. Mim had even witnessed some flirty interactions between nurses and their patients which made her blush. But now Mim was locked in a room with a patient who was so heavily sedated it was like being in solitary confinement. She was determined no one would judge her care of this man as unprofessional; this patient would absolutely get the best that she could offer... even if she was well and truly in over her head... and even if that meant she needed to talk with a barely conscious patient, to keep her sanity.

Mim stood up and went over to the bed. She tidied the sheets again, even though he had not moved. "Well, this is an unusual assignment that I have been given..." she said to the bandages. "I am here, at your beck and call for as long as you need. My name is Mim. Miriam really. Nurse Miriam Hillman at your service. As of now, you and me... we are best friends." She went to the cupboard to familiarised herself with the supplies. She opened the cedarwood wardrobe that had been crudely fitted with shelves. She checked off the array of items out loud: "Here we have one set of bedsheets; two spare towels; a few bandages; a dressing tray; a pair of pyjamas... these are hospital pyjamas – we can tell because the top and bottoms do not match; and there is a set of civilian clothes. That, I must say, is the drabbest brown suit I have ever seen. We might be able to get dressed up for dinner when you are feeling better. Well, that is the end of the inventory. A little sparse, don't you think? But we are, after all, a nation at war."

That became her routine... she would give this anonymous man a bright commentary on what she was doing, and why.

That evening, Mim was mopping the floor when the hatch opened, and their dinner tray was delivered. Mim sat the tray down by the patient and proceeded to gravity feed the syringe with some very thin broth through his tube. She poured herself a cup of tea, and as she lifted her cup, there, on the tray, was tucked a note from Marlie in the Kitchen: *"Dear Nurse. I have heard about your assignment, and I want to let you know you are in our prayers. If there is anything that you need, please add a note into the utensils pocket on your tray as it is returned and I will get it to you if it is within my ability to do so. Also... if you have some favourite food... (and I know rations are dominating the menu), but I would try my very best. Marlie (cook)."*

Sweet Marlie had no idea that it was Mim who was allocated this quarantine case. She quickly wrote a reply. "Dear Marlie, your letter means the world to me. I'm not sure you realise it is Mim (Miriam – of previous governess fame) who has been assigned this duty. I only had the opportunity to quickly bring the most basic supplies. If you could find some sort of salve as my hands are dry. I would seriously appreciate the daily newspaper to keep abreast of the outside world, and if you could retrieve these book titles, my life will be saved...". She tucked the note into the pocket that held the utensils.

Later that evening, the hatch opened, a newspaper and a couple of books were pushed through the slot. "This duty might not be too bad after all," she confessed to her patient as she put the books on her desk. "It is to my advantage that I am an introvert by nature." There was a tub of some sort of homemade grease, to which Marlie had attached a note. "This salve is my grandmother's recipe. Unfortunately, it smells unpleasant, but it works a treat. Just experiment and see how it works for you and your patient. You might be surprised."

Mim opened the lid and blinked with a grimace. That was not great. So, she set it aside and focused on the task at hand. "The time has come," she said to her patient. "Yes, the time has come to give you a name. It is against my nature to nurse a nameless body, so this will be my next mission. I am undecided how to go about this. I have never needed to name anything before, really, outside a doll my mother made for my sixth birthday. I named it Beatrix for not so obvious reasons. My parents thought it was an affectionate tribute to Beatrix Potter because I read her stories over and over. More accurately, (and I didn't want to tell my Mum this), her doll looked like Farmer McGregor. Glasses and all. All that was missing was the rake!" She laughed. "Huh. I've never confessed that to anyone before! But I do believe wholeheartedly that names are important, and I want to do this properly. I could give you a favourite name... like naming a baby. Or I could give you a symbolic name... something generic representing who I expect you are, or what your family might hope for... something grand, like Maximillian... a Roman conqueror, a fighter. You are a solider after all. And it looks like you put up a grand fight. Brave and devoted. There used to be a classic Roman bust in the Grandfield library here... and I always thought his carved marble features looked like a Maximillian – the name means "The Greatest!". Or... I could suggest some of my favourite books and we can find a character that is befitting of you..."

So Mim went through a list of her familiar characters to find a suitable pseudonym. Mr Darcy... that was overdone. Mr Rochester. Heathcliff. Gabriel Oak or Gilbert Blythe. So, this became her challenge. To find a name. In the end she decided that the choices were between Jane Eyre's Mr Rochester (rich and obnoxious); Emma's Mr Knightley (rich and well-mannered); and Dickens' Bob Cratchit (poor and loyal). She experimented with the sound of the names and decided they all went with Maximillian quite adequately: Maximillian Rochester, Maximillian Knightley or Maximillian Cratchit. "There is nothing else for it, Maximillian," she said to the bandages in the end, "but for me to read these stories to you, and I will allow you to decide." She smiled to herself as her patient lay there still and unresponsive.

So, while doing her nursing tasks, and the housekeeping chores required of their single hospital room, Mim started to read some of her favourite excerpts. *"There was no possibility of taking a walk that day... the cold winter wind had brought with it clouds so sombre, and a rain so penetrating, that further out-door exercise was now out of the question..."* She paused and considered the bandages lying in the bed. "You see, we will get along with Jane Eyre quite adequately... she was also locked in. I confess books have long been my escape." And Mim continued to read. She discussed her chosen excerpts as she went... sometimes propping the book on the bedside cabinet by the lamp during the night, as she was doing particular tasks. Then she moved on from Jane to Emma. *'Emma Woodhouse, handsome, clever, and rich, with a comfortable home and happy disposition, seemed to unite some of the best blessings of existence...'.* Mim was quite harsh with her assessment of this character. "It is completely unfair how Emma had been given all this by her creator. I am pleased that Miss Austin didn't also make her perfect. That would have been too much. I find it is Emma's financial ease that makes her most inaccessible. I had comfort growing up... but in humble and unassuming ways... without a lot of money. I will admit that Knightley is endearing – a *'well-connected, sensible man with a cheerful manner'.* Even I must confess, that is pretty hard to pass up. Rochester, on the other hand, is less appealing; a man whom Jane Eyre describes as *'changeful and abrupt'.*"

By the time they got to look at Bob Cratchit, Mim had already made up her mind. "It seems like I would much rather look after someone whose *'threadbare clothes have been brushed up to look sensible'...* doing the best that he can, in difficult and oppressive circumstances. That holds more appeal than the ease of comfort that the Knightleys or Rochesters possess. I am satisfied," Mim declared as she unwrapped his bandages to dress the burns on his forearms. "For our little sojourn of recovery together, I hereby name you Maximillian Cratchit. The grand and the bland come together; the bold and the sold into service; the strong and the wronged. Mr Cratchit, it is my privilege to look after someone like yourself who is dedicated and devoted, regardless of your difficult circumstances."

* * *

Dr Redmond, rattling his key in the door, to review the patient and his chart at least three times a day, was her only other human contact. Early one the morning, before the light at the window had barely penetrated the sill, that familiar sound of his key in the lock stirred her as she was dozing on her bunk. She shook herself awake, rubbing her eyes. She yawned as the Doctor reviewed the chart and noted the patient's positive progress in general.

"You know, Sister, he is quite stable now. If you want to take half an hour and go for a walk around the garden, then I will stay and do my assessment here. Not too many around the grounds this early. Just remember to keep what you are doing under wraps; this man is officially not here. I'll stay with the patient – this room can be my little bit of respite from everything else going on out there."

"Thank you, Doctor! No disrespect to our patient, but it feels like seven years have passed already." She grabbed her cape and headed out the door.

Mim ran straight to the Glasshouse. There in the shadows of the early morning was the limping figure of her father, moving among his seedling trays, ranging from bare soil waiting for the seeds to push through the surface, to those almost ready for planting. "Dad! I am so glad you are here!" He turned around and his face lit up with relief.

"Mim! My Darling! Where have you been? No one would say anything. I have been so worried. I wondered if you had changed your mind

65

about overseas service and they had shipped you out. They have been saying that some nurses get their marching orders with no time to say goodbye. I have been praying so hard."

"Well... I'm not allowed to say what I'm doing, but you are right – I was given my marching orders without any notice. But I am safe and close... and I am okay."

"Oh no, you are not doing that infectious case are you? Here... at the House?"

Mim wobbled her head with a wink. "I cannot say what I am doing."

"Oh, My Sweet. I am so sorry. We heard that patient is insufferably difficult."

Mim laughed. "He is heavily sedated because of his burns. He is fine." She widened her eyes... and shrugged quickly... "I mean... I heard that was another rumour. Nobody knows for sure..."

"Of course... yes, nobody knows," he agreed returning her wink. "As long you are okay." And they lingered in their hug for a long while.

"I am truly doing well. Dad, tell me... are you?"

"Mostly. I worry that I won't be able to keep up the supply for Marlie. They want us to be pretty much self-supporting. But the number of extra beds they are putting in there, are quickly filling up. It adds up to a lot of food for a lot of people. I can only do what I can do."

"But you are doing a wonderful job. Look at all this. There are so many seedlings packed into this place ready for planting."

"The additional garden-beds we've made around the grounds seem justified now. Marlie has been helping me sort through what works best. I am planting more bulky foods... like cabbage and potatoes... and there's the large pumpkin patch out behind the stables."

Their visit was over too quickly, and Mim returned to her duties. Dr Redmond's early morning visits allowed them both to look forward to this respite in his garden shed. Her dad would have a cup of diluted herbal tea ready, made from Marlie's concoction of herbs in his garden, and they would sip and yawn, and catch up together before the dawn broke on yet another day.

* * *

7

"Sister, take down the bandages so I can inspect the progress of his wounds. Please... hold his head firm." The doctor started to unwrap the bandages across his shoulders, but they had crusted on.

"If I had known you wanted to see them now, I would have already started to soak them off," said Mim. She dressed his wound daily as part of his routine, soaking them off. She quickly placed a canvas cover under his torso to protect the sheets, drenched a towel in a bucket of water and wrapped it around his shoulders like a shawl. He was restless, so Mim spoke reassuringly. "Sorry Maximillian, Doctor's orders. He just wants to check your burns are healing. I think he will be pleased how they are progressing... just be patient with us."

"Maximillian?"

"Well Dr Redmond, you said I could call my patient anything I liked. So, I have chosen a pseudonym for him. Maximillian Cratchit. Maximillian was the nickname I gave the marble bust of a Roman Caesar I used to dust in the Grandfield library: a strong solider. And the name Cratchit, is from the story..."

"A Christmas Carol. Dickens."

"Yes Sir. Our patient looks like this soldier is fighting ghosts... and Cratchit was loyal and true through all of Scrooge's deliberations."

"Oh. Well, it is obvious you have taken some time to consider these matters."

Mim laughed. "Thinking is something that I have plenty of time to attend to, Doctor. That book, *A Christmas Carol* was given to me when I was a governess here, so to me it seems an appropriate reference point in many ways."

As the dressings soaked off, Mim frowned at red inflamed skin stretched over his wasted frame. He might not be a prisoner of war, but he had the look of one. His bones protruded prominently under his night shirt. Patches of bald scalp puckered as it met new pink granulating skin that ran along his temple where broken blisters and burns had seared across the side of his face, giving his face an uneven, odd look. The patient groaned and the doctor ordered some more laudanum. Mim measured the dose and syringed it through his gastric tube.

"Doctor, I have some homemade salve that might be of benefit. I brought it in for my own hands, but perhaps we could try it."

"Well, let's patch test it. If you have access to something in these times that might help, we can hardly refuse a trial."

"Is he going to be okay Doctor?" whispered Mim.

"As far as it depends on us, you know he will. He is a fighter – that is obvious. As unglamorous this new battle is, it will demand all his wits and strength to get through it. It is difficult to know if the injuries to his throat will cause ongoing troubles with swallowing and speech, but we will know more when we try to take the tube out to start oral fluids. He didn't need the intensive specialist surgery some cases have required. I have heard they've established a whole hospital in England dedicated to reconstructing faces, and noses and jaws, just so soldiers can eat. This new warfare has caused debilitating injuries on an unprecedented scale. Typical that it has taken a Kiwi to get results. They've set up a big old mansion house and turned it into a hospital... like this place, I guess. ANZACs making their mark on this war once more."

"I've read about Dr Gillies surgeries. The paper said he is getting some remarkable results. If you have any medical books on that type of work, I would appreciate the chance to study them." They irrigated his burns and covered them again with clean dressings. Mim was taking advantage of another person to talk with. "My father broke his ankle a while back. Warehouse accident. Caring for him is what sparked my interest in nursing. It was convenient working here because it was close to home. It is ironic that I have a job back here in this same house, looking after another broken leg, when my plan was always to get as far away from Grandfield as I could. It is like my destiny is bound up here and I might never escape."

* * *

Mim adjusted the covers and wiped out the bowl that she had been using and hung up the towels. She sat down by the bed and picked up his wrist to go through the range of movements that she did every day. She massaged his hands with Marlie's salve, extending and flexing, every joint, every finger. Ever so gently, she felt him squeeze her hand.

Mim gasped. "Maximillian! You're awake!"

He squeezed her hand again.

"Can you hear me? Is it clear?" There had had been so many doubts about how his hearing might be affected."

He squeezed her hand again.

"This is great news! Do you think you could try to talk?" She studied his face. "Just gently... try to make a sound..."

He breathed, and she felt him adjust his posture, so slightly. Then he shook his head. He squeezed her hand, short and sharp. It felt like a 'no'.

"Oh. That's okay Maximillian. We can try again in the future. Can you open your eyes? Just try it. See if you notice any light..."

His eyes blinked slowly.

"How is that? Can you see any shadows? Any light at all?"

A firm, short and sharp response pulsed in her hand.

"Oh Maximillian... I'm so sorry. It may improve in time...." She didn't know what else to say. It seemed to take away the excitement she felt to have him awake.

Then there was a pause... then pulse-pulse-pulse-pulse; pulse-squeeze.

"Oh! You are talking with me! You know Morse Code?"

He squeezed her hand again.

"Oh, I wish I knew what you were saying. Morse seems so complicated... except SOS of course. You know... I could learn the basics. I *will* learn! I will get hold of a signallers' codex for reference so we can talk."

He squeezed her hand. Short and sharp.

"You don't want me to learn? But wouldn't it be great if we could talk?"

He squeezed her hand firmly again. He didn't let the pressure go of her hand.

Mim focused on his face, trying to read his thoughts. "You want me to learn..."

Positive pressure.

"But you don't want me to get the codex..."

Short and sharp.

"Okay... then how am I going to understand what..."

He interrupted with more pressure.

"Oh of course. You are right. Why not? You can teach me. If you feel up to it, we can start now. Let's start at the beginning. What is the signal for the letter A?"

Pulse-squeeze. Mim wrote that down as a dot-dash.

"B."

Squeeze-pulse-pulse-pulse.

It took a couple of sessions to get through the entire alphabet, Mim confirming and jotting down the references. It was a jubilant moment of success to have a completed alphabet.

"Now... give me a message... and I will decode it. What is something that you would like to say to me?" Pulses and squeezes tapped through his hand. "Wow. That is fast! Can you give it to me again... slower?"

Squeeze; pulse-pulse-pulse-pulse; pulse-squeeze; squeeze-pulse; squeeze-pulse-squeeze. A longer pause... squeeze-pulse-squeeze-squeeze; squeeze-squeeze-squeeze; pulse-pulse-squeeze.

Mim wrote it down in dashes and dots... and then laboriously translated it from the code he had given her. "THANK YOU? Oh Maximillian... you are a gentleman. It is my pleasure."

He refused to release her hand. There was another message. That took longer for her to decode. "WHAT IS YOUR NAME"

"-- / .. / -- / MIM. But you know that already. It is different saying it this way though." That became her favourite message: two dashes; two dots; two dashes... just to hear him say her name.

"What will I call you?" she asked, waiting for him to press her hand.

"-- / .- / -..- / MAX"

She laughed, pulled her hand away and didn't let him finish. "So, you have been listening. You know I chose Maximillian Cratchit as your name!

But it is such a mouthful as a pseudonym. It would take three pages to tap your name. I didn't choose it with Morse in mind."

Squeeze-pulse-pulse... Mim laboriously decoded his long message:

"DO YOU HAVE SOMEWHERE ELSE TO BE"

"Huh. Well, I get your point. And I am glad you approve. Maximillian Cratchit it is. Certainly, better than Case File 7285."

* * *

"Good morning, Maximillian!" said Mim cheerily as she returned from her early morning walk with her dad, and Doctor Redmond left to finish his morning rounds. He was very pleased with the ointment patch tests, and they planned to use it more extensively across his scaring. The sun was fading the night sky and Mim pulled across the heavy drapes so light could penetrate the dim shadows of the room. She had rigged up a bell over Maximillan's bed, so he could ring if he needed anything, without risk of it being knocked over and lost in the covers. They started each day reading her Mum's bible and a prayer. During breakfast she read some of the newspaper to him. And then she would get him out of bed to sit in a chair for a short time before he went back to rest. But this morning, rather than the silent, compliant patient she was used to, he became agitated, and he knocked the bell, again and again. His arms and head twisted and thrashed. "Shh! Maximillian, I am here. What is it? What is wrong?" But the more she tried to talk to him, the more agitated he became. Out of desperation she grabbed his hand. "WHAT IS IT" As she signalled, he miraculously calmed.

"GOOD MORNING" he replied.

"PROBLEM" she tapped.

"NONE" he responded.

73

As she translated his message, she threw down her notepad in disgust. "There is nothing wrong? You just want to say, 'Good morning!' That is a pretty low sort of trick."

He started to thrash again.

She picked up his hand.

"NO TRICK" he tapped.

"Well, it seems like it to me!" And as soon as the words left her mouth, he started to thrash again. Then, as she reached for his hand, he settled. She held his hand lightly for a long time and said nothing. Eventually she took her pad and laboriously made out a message to give him.

"WHY CANT I TALK WITH YOU / YOU CAN OBVIOUSLY HEAR ME"

"PRACTICE"

She worked on another message. "YOU WANT ME TO PRACTICE MORSE CODE"

"YES"

So Mim submitted to this routine, frustrating and demanding, on top of her nursing duties. It became like a bootcamp. Unrelenting. Exhausting. It took effort to translate what she wanted to ask, and then transcribe and translate what he said back in return.

"THIS IS TOO HARD"

"YOURE GETTING IT"

"I WANT TO GIVE UP"

"I NEED TO TALK WITH YOU / KEEP GOING"

That was the motivation that pushed her to become conversant with this new language. Mim made a list of common phrases that she practiced until they were memorised, and her ability to tap quickly and smoothly was improving. She didn't stop speaking with him; the silence would have been too oppressive; but she spoke carefully and added dots and dashes to what she was saying as she sat by his bed and pressed his hand.

"I HAVE A QUESTION" he tapped one morning.

"YES"

"WHAT IS THAT SMELL"

Mim laughed. "MARLIES OINTMENT / SMELLS TERRIBLE / BUT YOUR SKIN IS HEALING BETTER NOW / DOCTOR WANTS TO KEEP USING IT"

He nodded. He was quiet for a time, then he pressed her hand again. "DONT TELL ANYONE YOU KNOW MORSE"

"WHY NOT" Mim went still. Suddenly the war had truly penetrated this little cell. She had never clarified with him his role, and why he was here before. Not knowing seemed easier. "ARE YOU A PRISONER" Was he asking her to betray her country?

He smiled at that. "IT FEELS LIKE IT" Their cell was occupied by nurse and patient, incarcerated together. "ALLY / SOLDIER"

So not a P.O.W. The Doctor had suggested that the individual care the army was expecting would ordinarily suggest rank, but he denied any. "WHY ARE YOU GETTING ALLOCATED CARE IF YOU HAVE NO RANK"

"SIGNALLER / INTERCEPTED INTEL" Mim looked at him and shook her head. She still didn't understand. He kept tapping. "I WANT YOU TO WRITE DOWN SOME MESSAGES / DON'T TELL ANYONE ABOUT IT / THAT IS WHY YOU COULD NOT ASK FOR A CODEX / YOU MUST NOT TELL ANYONE I HAVE SAID

ANYTHING / IT IS FOR YOUR OWN SAFETY" Any scrap notes she made, even translating as she was learning, were to be burnt in the fireplace.

"THEN WHY TELL ME ANYTHING AT ALL"

"IN CASE SOMETHING HAPPENS / CONFIDENTIAL / IMPORTANT TO THE WAR". He gave instructions on what she must do with his notes if he suddenly died.

"BE CERTAIN I WILL DO EVERYTHING I CAN TO MAKE SURE THAT DOESN'T HAPPEN"

Maximillian dictated his messages patiently, cryptic and obscure. Mim had very little insight into what any of it meant or how it could have an impact on things going on in a war halfway around the world. Yet she followed his instructions precisely and filed the messages in a particular order; secured in a place hidden behind the bottom drawer of the hutch. Every day another detail was added to the growing body of war intelligence in that secret file.

While she tapped and wrote and decoded and double checked, deep down Mim had a realisation: she had wanted Maximillian to be, not a Cratchit, but a Knightley or Rochester. Rich and positioned, mannerly or obnoxious aside. She still craved the fantasy of an influential and positioned man, one with money and reputation who would come and sweep her onto his gallant steed. Then they would ride off and fight wars together. In her romantic view of the world, this was better than being placed through solid character, sacrifice, hard work. Being a foot-soldier, wounded in a war that was fighting to preserve something worthwhile was not at all glamorous. This was a painful insight of the way she was looking at this war, and the people caught in its talons. This was especially true since she had grown up in a home with these simple values of solid character, sacrifice, and hard work. It was a rebuke to realise how tightly she held onto these superficial measures. Private Maximillian Crotchet, a cot-case soldier, was saved, not due to rank, or position, or net-worth, but merely because fate had determined that somehow, he would hold enemy secrets. The powers that sanctioned his care wanted those secrets and couldn't care less about the soldier. That broke her heart. To Mim it was the other way around: the secrets were immaterial and the man she nursed was valued. Poor and loyal. That was worth so much more than any espionage secret, any rank or file, any peerage or lubricating income.

* * *

8

Mim frowned soberly and went over to the service-cord hanging by the wall. Once, she was one of the staff who was summoned by its demanding tinkle. Now she was appealing for help to come to her. She had used this bell a few times, but today it was critical. She paced, going back and forth, between the open medical volume on her desk, and Mr Cratchit who was dozing fitfully on his bed. He lay there, unaware that another bomb had just exploded on his life. She was praying as she tracked that circuit again, waiting for Doctor Redmond to come. She went back to the cord and pulled it again.

Doctor Redmond opened the door with a frown framing his spectacles. Mim handed him the chart, lifted the covers so he could inspect his leg. He paused, his lips thinning in a sombre line, his frown deepened as he prodded and calculated adjustments to his schedule for that day. "I will be back with an assistant to amputate this afternoon. You are correct Nurse: this is gangrene, and it cannot be postponed. If we are lucky, we can hold it to below the knee. The bone was so badly shattered it was a long shot at best. It is a good thing we have crossed your blood with his, so be prepared: we may need to do a transfusion. Move your bunk so we can do that if needed. You know the other things that are needed to get ready."

* * *

Mim put away the mop and wiped over the bedside table again, took his pulse and temperature, changed the bottle of Ringer's solution and added dressings to stump of his leg. She sighed and sat down. She felt lightheaded and weak, and poured herself a drink of Marlie's lemonade as she nibbled on a biscuit from a stash that she kept for emergency snack attacks.

She had hoped that his multiple broken bones would mend... but an amputated leg could never grow back. That was now a hope that no longer existed. She heard her father's voice in her head, *'Glad they didn't chop my foot off. Never seen anyone come through that very well,'* he had said. "Well," Mim determined, "Maximillian Cratchit – you are going to be the exception." Over and over, she reminded herself that she had saved his life, but it still felt like she had let him down. Personally, and professionally, she had failed. In some way, it was her leg that had been taken. It had been a small matter to see her blood run through the tubes to his arm. And she wondered how angry Mr Cratchit would be when he came to and really understood what had happened.

It seemed to take much longer than the doctor expected for him to improve. Their routine every day still started with reading her mother's Bible, tapping out the words as she read. More than ever, she needed the wisdom of God with her, infusing her and her patient with hope; praying that God would restore this man, inside and out. She used code all the time, pressing his hand, trying to get a response. But his hand lay limp. She took up her storybooks again and read Jane Eyre from the beginning. And then, because it was a seasonal story, she followed with A Christmas Carol and told him the story of how she had come by the book, and why it was something that she held affectionately in her list of prized possessions. The New Year came in with her sitting vigil by his bed. Days blurred.

* * *

One morning Dr Redmond missed coming in to relieve Mim for her early morning tea with her dad; she was pacing the floor when an older, portly doctor finally arrived with an army officer. "What has happened to Dr Redmond? Is he well?" Mim asked concerned.

This doctor had a large handlebar moustache and spoke with a wheeze. He shook his grey head with an impatient sigh. "He was attacked by one of the in-patients. Serious. I don't expect he will be back. Inconvenient to say the least. I am now the supervising medic... working between four places now. So, I won't be moddy-coddling you like Redmond did. The Sergeant here, has a couple of questions about the patient since Redmond is out of the picture." The Officer stepped forward and impatiently demanded to know if the patient had discussed anything with her; disclosed any war information.

Mim shook her head vaguely. "Sir, I'm sure Dr Redmond would have told you that this patient cannot speak due to his throat injuries. His recovery since the surgery has been slow. However, he is starting to respond, and I am very hopeful that this improvement will mean that he will soon be coherent and strong enough to write things down." If this man's secrets were the only reason that they valued him, then Mim was going to ensure that information was his currency to getting appropriate care. Without the hope of gaining military secrets, Mim suspected the incentive to keep him alive would rapidly wane and they would just as quickly discard him completely.

The officer sniffed at the smell in the room; the odour from the ointment now pervaded everything. Mim realised she had become immune to its fumes. He growled at her again, insistent that disclosures of intelligence be made directly to him. Mim picked up his chart and handed it to him. "Sir, I am his only nurse, and I can assure you that this man is a solider through and through. He is a fighter, and this has been demonstrated by his progress since his admission as a cot case. This is another battle he is fighting, and he is committed. He got through that, and I am confident he will get through this. I have no other information I can offer you."

The officer scowled, slapped the chart on the trolly and left the room. His abrupt tread hitting the hard floors down the hall as he left, muttering to the doctor who followed him outside, panting to keep up his pace.

Accusations about the room smelling like a pigpen added to the inadequacy of the situation, fading as their voices retreated down the corridor.

After the door abruptly shut, Mim stood in the middle of the room for quite a while. She took some slow breaths and then turned to resume her duties. Her hand was trembling as she took his pulse. Barely perceivably she felt him shift his grip to squeeze her hand. "THANK YOU"

She quickly looked at his face, but his lids were still and his face unmoved.

"HOW ARE YOU FEELING" She could see his brow furrow as he focussed on her message.

"RUN OVER BY A TRUCK"

"REST", she responded, and then adjusted his pillow and smoothed his covers, and wet his lips and mouth with very small drops of water.

He found her hand again. "BIG ARMY TRUCK"

She smiled and squeezed his hand affectionately. He barely nodded, before he dozed off. Mim sat looking at him for a long time: his cheekbones prominent; his eye sockets sunken and the red scar tissue along the left side of his face and neck was fading as she diligently applied the ointment, but it was still stretched taut over his frame. His beard was rough and unruly that he refused to allow her to trim; the bald patches along his hairline were hollow and lop-sided. His collarbones protruded from his frame in a way that reminded her of the nursing lectures with the clinical skeleton, Mr Bones, who had taught them the names of each bony structure of the body. Yet this prisoner had become an extension of herself, fused as a bond slave to whatever his life might be. "You will be okay, Mr Cratchit," she whispered as he slept. "I sincerely believe that."

* * *

9

"GET ME A PAD"

"WHAT FOR"

"I HAVE TO GIVE THAT OFFICER SOMETHING TO JUSTIFY ME BEING HERE / IF HE THINKS I AM STARTING TO DISCLOSE INTELEGENCE HE WILL KEEP ME HERE / I CANNOT RISK HIM WIPING ME OFF"

Mim grabbed a pad and a pencil. Maximillian made a few illegible scratches across the page. "TELL HIM I WAS AGGITATED AND THE NEED TO WRITE WAS URGENT / AND MAKE A COPY"

Mim laughed. "I actually am looking forward to him coming again. I have only dreaded his complaining about the smell of the room, stomping around and demanding I make you rise up and walk."

Mim folded the paper and sealed it in an envelope. She told the Doctor as he darted in for his daily rounds, that she had something for the Army Officer. The Doctor demanded to see it, but Mim stood resolute. "Doctor, I will only pass this on in person as the officers have been very clear that any change in status was to be reported directly to him."

It was not long before the officer appeared. Mim handed him the envelope. "Sir, I think it is important. The patient became very agitated. When I gave him the notepad, his need to write seemed very urgent. I'm not sure it makes sense, but there is a marked improvement. I will continue to offer him a pad as he has is having more lucid periods."

Every few days there was another envelope. The scratchings varied, but more letters were added, and then gradually the occasional word was included. Maximillian still insisted Mim kept a copy of the messages and sighed. "I DOUBT THEY REALISE PUTTING THESE TOGETHER WILL GIVE A MESSAGE / IT STARTS / *AN IMPORTANT MESSAGE FOR THE WAR OFFICE / TO WHOM IT MAY CONCERN*"

"THAT IS HOW YOU STARTED THE OTHER MESSAGES"

"ONE AND THE SAME / AT SOME POINT WE MAY HAVE TO HELP THEM DECIPHER IT"

His strength improved. One night, Mim went out on the general ward and brought back a wheelchair. "Shh. I thought we might play hooky and go for a spin around the garden. I am quite happy to diagnose you have cabin-fever, since I am certain that I also am afflicted, so to get outside is as therapeutic as anything else we do."

She quietly wheeled him through the corridors, pausing to avoid the night nurses. He could feel the cool air as she opened the door. They paused for a moment on the landing and took it all in, breathing deeply. She wheeled him slowly down the ramp installed for the chairs and walking frames used by the patients to access the gardens.

She rested her hand on his shoulder. "ARE YOU DOING OKAY"

He reached up and touched her hand. "YES / KEEP GOING"

Min wheeled him out along the path, pausing every now and again, her hand on his shoulder.

He tapped. "TELL ME WHERE WE ARE"

"WE ARE ON THE WEST PATH / TOWARDS THE GLASSHOUSE / IT IS WHERE MY FATHER PLANTS HIS SEEDLINGS FOR THE VEGETABLE GARDEN / MARLIE USES HIS PUMPKINS FOR YOUR SOUP"

He titled his hand, listening to the night birds. "MOPOKE"

"YES / AND THAT HORRIFIC SCREECH IS A CURLEW"

"SOME CREATURES HAVE AN UNFORTUNATE VOICE / BUT AT LEAST THEY HAVE ONE"

"YOU HAVE A VOICE / I HEAR YOU"

They did a couple of laps and then Mim returned to their room. As she helped him back into his bed, he held her hand. "THANK YOU / THAT WAS A DOSE OF MEDICINE I DIDNT MIND TAKING / SMELT BETTER TOO"

A couple of nights later, at zero two thirty Maximillian rang his bell. Mim jumped up in a panic. It had been a long time since she was woken during the night apart from the set checks she had scheduled by the clock. "Maximillian – what is it?" she asked urgently as she lit the lamp.

"GET THE CHAIR / I NEED ANOTHER DOSE OF OUTSIDE"

"Oh. Okay then. Wait, I have to dress warmer if I am going outside."

It became something of a routine, two or three times a week they would sneak past the night staff and venture outside.

* * *

"Right, Mr Cratchit, we are going to walk around the bed today using your new leg."

"NO"

"No?" Mim shook her head and took his hand. "WHAT DO YOU MEAN NO / YOU HAVE TO TRY" Her tapping was emphatic.

"NO I DONT"

She abandoned tapping and spoke firmly. "Although you have had it fitted, you have refused to try walking with it. You need to do this with the same determination that you have shown in swallowing without the gastric-tube. And what about the determination that taught me Morse? This is the next thing. Do it or I will…"

"OR WHAT"

"Or… I will not talk to you apart from what is needed for my job."

"BUMPKIM"

"I will!"

"I LIKE SILENCE" He scowled and pressed his lips in a grim line that suggested that this was a dare he was willing to take.

She smartly tapped back. "AND OUTSIDE EXCURSIONS ARE HEREBY SUSPENDED"

"YOU ARE GROUNDING ME / FINE / DOESNT CHANGE MY MIND" His tapping was sharp. He scowled, his manner gruff, dark, irate, and piercing – just as Jane Eyre described her Rochester.

Mim shook her head and turned away. Of course, she would call him on matters that were not best for his health. "Rochester! Can't you just be willing to try?"

Mim stepped back. Would he relent once he understood she would not meekly wave a white flag? He needed to do this. He had said that he liked talking with her and she wondered how true this declaration was. She lifted his prosthesis onto the bed. "LEG", she tapped very clearly.

"NO" he replied. His face was surly, and his tapping was still sharp and emphatic.

She paused, picked up the prosthetic and propped it up against the wardrobe without an argument, then silently helped him with his crutches, doing laps around the bed hopping on one leg. She went about her observations and cleaning duties without her usual chatter. When she read the weekly newspaper – rather than reading out-loud, she read quietly to herself, making sure she rustled the pages, so he knew exactly what she was doing. She helped him with his liquid meals without the banter or the small talk that had been their routine. As she supported his hand holding the cup of thin soup to his lips, she decided that his wasted body needed a more robust diet. When she stacked away her dishes on the tray, she wrote to Marlie explaining the need to strengthen her patient's nutrition, requesting thicker bone-broths, vegetable soups (run through a sieve) and egg custards.

He raised his brow when he tasted the rich bone-broth. The thicker consistency seemed easier to swallow. There was much less spluttering. "THANKS"

Mim tapped a formal "NOTED" in reply. Twice a day she tapped, "LEG" and put it away when he declined; and she helped him use the crutches. The new improved diet made an impression and Cratchit gave a rating after every meal. When there was a particular soup that he like he would tap "4", less favoured versions were given one or two taps. Once, this would have given them a rich field of conversation, but now Mim only replied with a formal "NOTED". She faithfully passed his feedback on to Marlie, and soon they had introduced a variety of nutritious options that were more to his taste.

After two weeks, when she tapped "LEG" that evening, he responded with "TOMORROW". It was humiliating to acknowledge it took him so little time to relent. But she was right. It was something he needed to do. He might as well get it over with.

Mim let out a deep sigh and realised the whole time had been like holding her breath. "Oh! Finally!" she enthused. "I am so relieved! You have no idea how hard this has been for me. You are a very stubborn man, so I am very grateful that you have decided to give it a try. We will take it slowly, but I promise you, we will have you running marathons without your crutches in the manner of the ancient Greek athletes in no time."

He shook his head. "CHATTERBOX / MIGHT GO BACK TO THE SILENCE" he responded with a wry shake of his head.

Mim looked at him. Another time when someone else accused her of being a chatterbox flashed before her eyes. Perhaps it was her way. "Okay. Noted. Well, Mr Cratchit, you can let me know if I talk too much and I will wind it back. I have proven that I can."

He shrugged. "I THINK WE JUST HAD OUR FIRST ARGUMENT / YOU WON"

Mim laughed at that. "I am glad we are friends again."

When Mim woke in the morning, she felt a stir of excitement. She sensed that Cratchit was turning a corner. They went through their morning routines reverting to the comfortable banter and conversation they had become familiar with. "ARE YOU READY TO TRY YOUR LEG NOW OR DID YOU WANT TO REST FIRST"

"TRY NOW"

Mim smoothed the knitted sock over his stump and strapped the leather buckles on and patiently adjusted the tension for his comfort. Mim placed a chair in front, and on each side of him so he could stand, weight bearing using the backs of the chairs for support. She looked at him holding on to the chairs, bent and uncertain. "You know – you strike a rather imposing figure. If we put you in a uniform, no one would ever know."

His thin, drawn face did not move, but he tapped on the chair as he lent forward. "FLATTERY NOTED"

"I am quite serious Mr Cratchit. We will find a way to manage these limitations so you can get on with your life." His mouth barely twitched. "THIS TIME WE STEP", she tapped on his shoulder. She watched his face closely as he tried to distribute his weight and shuffle forward. After a few minutes he signalled to return to bed. "WELL DONE" she responded warmly. "A MOMUMENTAL SUCCESS"

"HARDLY"

"IT TAKES A WHILE" She supported him back to bed and adjusted his covers. "It might seem like nothing much, but today you have achieved something you have never done before. That, Mr Cratchit, should not be underestimated."

"FLATTERY NOTED / AGAIN"

"It is not flattery if it is the truth. I am quite genuine, and if I have any agenda, it is just to see you well. You have a life, Mr Cratchit, outside these walls. And it is my intention that you get to experience it with every possible advantage."

He laid back on his pillows and was soon breathing regularly in sleep, fatigued from his efforts.

* * *

Each day they took more steps, and Mim shuffled the chairs forward for support. They practiced until they were walking around the room, using only his stick, practicing turns and pausing, and starting over.

One night, Mim woke to the bell ringing. She lit the lamp and check the clock. Zero two thirty. "Maximillian – what is it?" She yawned widely.

"GET THE CHAIR / TAKE ME OUTSIDE / I AM GOING FOR A WALK"

"IT IS THE MIDDLE OF THE NIGHT / WALKING OUTSIDE IS VERY DIFFERENT TO TAKING THE CHAIR"

"YES IT IS"

He could not be serious. "IT IS DARK"

"I AM BLIND / IT IS ALWAYS DARK / TAKE A LAMP IF YOU MUST"

"Oh. Okay..."

She wheeled him down the ramp and parked the chair by one of the garden seats. He stood and found his balance tapping his stick as they moved slowly forward. They walked up and back.

"LET ME SIT"

She guided him back to the bench where they sat for a time in silence, blanketed in the muted quiet of night, punctuated by the curlew and mopoke.

"TAKE ME BACK NOW" he said as he stood and reached for the chair. She wheeled him along the path, back inside.

* * *

Mim handed the Doctor another envelope since the officer had declared it was a waste of his time to come into the hospital for a series of scribbles. He stood at the end of the bed and frowned as Cratchit lay on the bed weakly lifting his limp hand. "Nurse, you said he was getting stronger. Why isn't he up and about more?"

Mim swallowed. Maximillan had been clear that he wanted her to be cautious about disclosing his progress. Still, she felt defensive that they were using his lack of 'progress' to reflect poorly on her work ethic. And skill. She was applying everything she was trained to do. She wasn't passively sitting by his bed. She *was* working hard. "I think we need try foods that are a little more substantial. The nutrition will support his overall energy levels. It is good that he is trying the artificial limb on, but he is reluctant to move."

The doctor frowned. "Whatever you think. The Army is getting edgy about this patient. They are frustrated by his scribbles. But until he is eating and moving, we can't seriously contemplate discharge."

"I am doing my best Doctor," said Mim firmly.

The doctor left and Mim sat on the bed – a rather unprofessional gesture that would never be allowed anywhere else in the hospital. Being locked away in a room had its advantages. "CARE TO EXPLAIN" she tapped. "YOU ARE MAKING MUCH BETTER PROGRESS THAN YOU LET ON / WHY DO WE HAVE TO HIDE THIS"

"I NEED TIME / I MUST KNOW I CAN MANAGE"

"OKAY / BUT YOU NEED TO DRIVE THIS / OTHERWISE I TITTLETAT"

"JUDAS"

"NO / I AM YOUR GREATEST ALLY"

* * *

"Cratchit!" Mim woke to find her patient not in his bed. As she flew around the bed; he was on the floor determinedly doing push ups. "What are you doing?"

He paused and sat up, and his hair flopped over his blind eyes. He tapped. "15"

"Do you do this every morning?" she asked astounded. How could she not know?

This had been his nightly routine after their laps around the grounds for a while now. He waited until after Mim collapsed into bed. "GETTING

90

STRONGER" he said confidently, and he told her he was increasing his sets to twice a day, working towards three times a day.

Mim grinned. "I'll do them with you."

They talked about his diet and his struggle to swallow solid food. They trialled more substantial food other than soup... soft foods like mashed pumpkin. They made a list of what caused him to gag, and what he could tolerate in small portions. Another step forward.

* * *

The officer stood impatiently by the door. "This had better be important. Has it started any coherent writing?"

"Perhaps... I'm not sure."

"You're not sure! What does that even mean? I am a very busy man!"

"Yes, yes Sir, I appreciate that. But I wanted to show you something." Mim pointed to a copy of all the notes that had been given to the officer, numbered and lined up on her desk. "I don't have a lot to entertain myself in here. I confess I was a little bored, and I wondered what he was writing, as it always seemed so urgent. I think there is more to what he was writing than random scratchings. Of course, your team may already be aware of this..." She handed over the final sheet where she had translated his random marks onto a single sheet, and under the lines she had smoothly written the deciphered message: 1917 *An important message for the Australian War Office: To whom it may concern...*"

The officer stared at the sheets. Swore. Glanced at the patient sleeping in the bed, deliriously moving around the bed in his restlessness. In a single sweep he gathered all the numbered pages from her desk, turned on his heel, and disappeared, slamming the door behind him.

Mim quietly locked the door and then sat by his bed. "I THINK HE WAS IMPRESSED"

Maximillian grinned. "YEP / THEY MISSED THAT / WE HAVE BOUGHT SOME TIME"

* * *

The nightly excursions were a routine of walking and walking and walking laps around the grounds. The small circle of light from the little lamp that she carried bounced in time with their steps as they walked. They would then choose a bench and sit for a time. The privilege of communicating in morse meant their conversations were always private. "ITS UNCANNY HOW YOU WAKE UP IN THE MIDDLE OF THE NIGHT WITHOUT AN ALARM CLOCK" Mim carried a pencil in her pocket, that she used for tapping on his knee.

He tapped her hand with his finger. "ARMY TRAINING / SIGNALLERS NEED TO ORIENTATE TO TIME WITHOUT A WATCH / THEY WOULD ALLOCATE A TIME AND DO SPOT CHECKS / ANYONE STILL ASLEEP WAS GIVEN PICKET DUTY / THAT MEANS PICK UP ALL THE CRAP AROUND CAMP / WE GOT GOOD AT AVOIDING THAT / GIVE ME A TIME / I CAN WAKE UP"

"I STILL NEED AN ALARM"

Then they would do another set of laps before resting on a bench in the night shadows. Mim turned down the lamp. It conserved fuel and the dark was not difficult for her either.

"TELL ME ABOUT YOUR LIFE AT GRANDFIELD" Cratchit said. "BEFORE NURSING / WHAT WAS IT LIKE BACK THEN"

Mim considered his question as she looked back towards the grand old house standing tall against the dark, star-studded sky lit only by a slither of moon. The city in black-out felt like they were miles away from their neighbours. The fragrance of flowering jasmine blended with all the other of memories that she had of these grounds, when she snatched time with her father working in the garden.

"I WAS THE GOVERNESS / GOT THE POSITION AFTER MY MUM DIED"

"HOW DID YOU GET THE JOB".

"MRS WHITAKER TOOK ME ON AS A FAVOUR TO MY MOTHERS EMPLOYER / MUM LOVED WORKING FOR THAT LADY / THEY WERE FRIENDS"

"HOW DID SHE DIE"

"TUBERCULOSIS / IT WAS AWFUL / THEN DAD HAD HIS ACCIDENT AND COULDN'T WORK / THE MEDICAL BILLS WERE A LOT SO WE HAD TO SELL OUR HOME"

"IM SORRY"

"I STILL MISS HER"

"IS THAT WHY YOU CHOSE NURSING"

"SORT OF / MORE A PRAGMATIC CHOICE / I LOOKED AFTER MY DAD WHEN HE WAS INJURED / SOMEONE ONCE CHALLENGED ME TO DO MORE THAN GOVERNESSING / HE SAID I HAD MORE IN ME"

"HE / WAS HE YOUR BOYFRIEND"

"NO / JUST A FRIENDLY ENCOUNTER / BUT WHAT HE SAID STUCK WITH ME"

"I WISH I WAS HIM"

"NO YOU DON'T / YOU ARE A MUCH BETTER PERSON THAN HIM / HE WAS RICH AND ARROGANT / NURSING SEEMED TO FIT / ANYWAY I ENDED UP BACK HERE AT GRANDFIELD / DIDNT EXPECT THAT"

"THATS IRONIC"

"DESTINY PERHAPS"

"PERHAPS / AND YOUR CHARGE / WHAT WAS SHE LIKE"

"ANNA WHITAKER"

"ANNA / NICE NAME" He sighed deeply as he said it.

"ANNA WAS PRETTY / BRIGHT / PRECOCIOUS / SMART / SOMETIMES INSOLENT / MOSTLY CHARMING AND BOLD / I LIKED HER"

"WAS SHE SPOILT"

"DEFINITELY / BUT NOT HER FAULT"

"WHERE IS SHE NOW" His tapping was cautious; tentative.

"NOT SURE / I HEARD SHE DEFIED HER PARENTS TO GO NURSING / BUT SHE DIDNT COME BACK HERE AFTER HER TRAINING / MARLIE STILL KEEPS IN TOUCH / SHE IS OKAY AS FAR AS I KNOW"

"WHY NOT NURSE HERE / THIS WAS HER HOME"

"STAFF GRAPEVINE SUGGESTS THAT WAS THE MAIN REASON"

"WHY DID YOU COME BACK"

"TO BE WITH MY FATHER / HE IS MY ONLY FAMILY / SINCE HIS ACCIDENT HE WALKS SLOWLY WITH A LIMP /

THAT IS NOTHING NOW / BUT BACK THEN IT WAS A VERY GENEROUS APPOINTMENT"

"DO YOU SEE HIM OFTEN"

"DOCTOR REDMOND USED TO RELEIVE ME EVERY MORNING / THE NEW GUY DOESNT"

Night after night, the pages were turned on their inner lives. There were two things Cratchit refused to talk about: the war, and his family. Mim resolved to be satisfied with the things he had conceded to share.

One night as they sat on the bench listening to the night birds; a barking owl yapped its 'roof-roof". It was drizzling rain, and she shifted her weight and adjusted her slicker and cape. "I AM SURPRISED YOU WANTED TO COME OUT IN THE RAIN" she tapped on his knee, and he sat with his face turned to the sky, feeling the droplets on his face.

"I DO NOT MELT / WE WILL DRY"

"POINT TAKEN"

"I NEVER USED TO BE SO PARTIAL TO BEING OUTSIDE / NOW I FIND A WALK WITH GOOD COMPANY IS PLEASANT"

Good company? Mim was unable to contain her curiosity. "HAVE YOU EVER KEPT COMPANY WITH ANYONE BEFORE"

"MANY TIMES / NEVER LASTED / THEY WERE SPOILT / COULDNT BIDE BY IT" He turned his head towards her and tilted his head. "WHAT ABOUT YOU / DO YOU HAVE A BEAU"

She laughed quietly. "IM LOCKED IN A SINGLE ROOM DURING A WORLD WAR / THE OPPORTUNITY FOR DATING IS MIMIMAL"

"HAVE YOU EVER / BEFORE"

"I HAD AN INVITATION TO WALK TO CHURCH ONCE / IT WAS RAINING LIKE THIS / THE LONGEST MOST PAINFUL TEN MINUTES OF MY LIFE / VERY DISAPPOINTING"

"NOT LIKE OUR LAPS AROUND THE GROUNDS AT NIGHT / EVEN IN THE RAIN OUR WALKS NEVER LAST LONG ENOUGH"

Mim gasped. *What did he say?* Her mind raced. She stood and quickly picked up the lamp that had fizzled out in the rain, then hurried him back to the room in the dark. She had not realised until that moment what had happened.

** * **

10

"MIM"

"Yes," she sat down on the bed beside him, as was her habit. "What's going on? You seem serious."

"I AM"

"OH" She sat silently and held her breath. Since that realisation in the garden everything had changed. She never confessed anything to Maximillian outright, but she knew he felt it too. What she now understood was that he returned her affection. His touch seemed more tender; his manner so gentle. Perhaps this was to be the moment of complete disclosure. "WHAT IS IT"

"IT IS TIME TO GET READY TO SAY GOODBYE"

"No! You cannot!" she gasped.

"I KNOW WE CAN BECAUSE I HAVE THAT 'QUEER FEELING AS IF I HAVE A STRING SOMEWHERE UNDER MY LEFT RIBS TIGHTLY AND INEXTRICABLY KNOTTED TO A SIMILAR STRING SITUATED IN THE CORRESPONDING QUARTER OF YOUR LITTLE FRAME'"

Mim closed her eyes and felt Rochester's words from the page of her book come to life, as she felt his hand tattoo them into her heart as he tapped.

Was discharge and separation even a realistic option? Unquestionably his condition demanded more support, more time. "SURELY NOT YET / YOU ARE NOT READY / I AM NOT READY"

"I HAVE TESTED EVERY ASPECT / ALTHOUGH MY EATING IS NOT GREAT IT IS PROBABLY THE BEST I CAN ANTICIPATE"

"ARE YOU SURE"

"IT IS TIME TO FINISH WHAT I STARTED"

Mim felt the lump in her throat grow so large that she could barely swallow. She blinked hard and felt her tears as they refused to stay contained. Instinctively he reached out and gently wiped them with his sleeve, his silence saying more than words.

Slowly she calmed and resolved to be brave. "I WOULD EXPECT NO LESS FROM YOU MR CRATCHIT" Of course. Mr Cratchit – poor and loyal, would finish what was required of him, until it was done. "WHAT DO YOU NEED FROM ME" She tapped slowly, forcing the letters to form words.

"HAIRCUT AND BEARD TRIM / THATS A GOOD START" The rest he would manage when he was back in uniform.

She sat still, her eyes closed, trying to imprint the feel of his hand in hers. Just like Jane Eyre, there was an invisible string that would always connect her to her Rochester. Their grip was that string that had become the tubing where her blood flowed into his veins, sharing life. But she knew it went both ways. His blood supported her life too.

"MIM"

"YES"

"GET YOUR SISSORS"

She released his hand and quietly stood up. "Yes Sir," she said quietly. He sat on the chair, and she wrapped a towel around his shoulders. He was no longer so emancipated, but he was still thin, still gaunt. She ran a comb gently through his hair and paused as he winced when she touched the tender scar tissue on his scalp.

He reached out and touched her arm. Mim jolted and then focused as he tapped. "TIDY BUT NOT MILLITARY SHORT"

"But you going back to the army. You said so..."

"YES / BUT I LEAVE AS MAXIMILLIAN CRATCHIT / NOT CASE FILE 7285"

She swallowed hard. "Yes Sir," she murmured. "I will try."

"YOU ARE DOING GREAT"

"Did you want a shave?"

"TRIM"

She felt his breath on her face as she focused on trimming his beard evenly around his jaw. "I was right..." she murmured. "You do strike a rather imposing figure, and no one will ever know what you have been through unless you choose to tell them."

"YOU KNOW IT ALL"

"I do Sir. You have been through a lot."

"IT MEANS SO MUCH THAT YOU WERE HERE"

"Thank you... Maximillian," she said swallowing hard, tears falling on the towel as she reached out and placed his hand on his beard. "Is this short enough?"

He ran his hand over his beard and up through his hair line and nodded. He reached out for her, and she placed her hand in his. "I..." he started to tap, and then he stopped. "THANK YOU FOR EVERYTHING / I AM GRATEFUL" He squeezed every signal slowly. He took her hand a pressed it to his lips.

"THE FILE OF MESSAGES / DO YOU NEED THEM"

"YES"

She went to the wardrobe and pulled out the bottom drawer and retrieved the file from behind the cavity. It was filled with the papers that documented all that he had shared. "Sir, you are a man with secrets who could hold many to ransom," she said quietly as she pressed the envelope into his hands.

He tapped back. "THAT IS THE MAN I AM GOING TO SAY GOODBYE TO"

The door opened and the doctor came in. He looked about the room. The bed was made in military precision. The patient was sitting in the chair in his civilian brown pants and jacket, his boots on both legs were smartly polished. A small bundle of toiletries and personal items were in a generic calico bag on the bedside table. A paper file was sitting on top of it. Mim stood stiffly by the end of the bed, her uniform starched.

Maximillian Cratchit smartly stood to his feet, his stick hitting the floor in a firm rap as he saluted and put his hand back by his side. The doctor thoughtfully considered the scene before him. "Case file 7285 reporting for duty I presume."

Maximillian nodded.

"Well, there is one particular officer who will be pleased to hear that. Nurse – have you attended to the discharge papers?"

"Most of it. Just waiting for your final clearance Doctor." Her voice crackled and she cleared her throat. "I have written a clear summary of his dietary requirements; his mobility needs and communication limitations. He will need some ongoing support with certain activities-of-daily-living due to his blindness."

"Well Nurse, it seems that your patient's recovery is miraculous. Yesterday he was barely able to sit up. Soldier – I trust your next assignment will be safe, and our country thanks you for your sacrifice and service. I will send a message to your commanding officer. They will be anxious to meet with you." He turned to leave and then paused. "Say your goodbyes. They will come and collect you from here. I expect they won't take long to get here. "Nurse, I am assigning you a full-week's leave when the discharge is finalised. After that, report back to the Ward Sister and she will give you your next allocation."

"Thank you, Doctor."

He left subdued, and turned the lock in the door after he closed the door, as was his habit.

"I DONT KNOW HOW TO SAY GOODBYE" Mim tapped gently.

"THEN DONT"

"THIS IS HARD / THE WAR HAS COME TO ME / MORE THAN I THOUGHT IT WOULD"

"YOU ARE A STRONG BRAVE REMARKABLE WOMAN MIM HILLMAN / I AM PRIVILIGED TO KNOW YOU"

"BE SAFE MAXILMIILIAN CRATCHIT / YOU ARE MY KNIGHTLEY"

A 'well-connected, sensible man with a cheerful manner'. Independent and likeable...

"REMEMBER ROCHESTERS STRING THAT CONNECTS OUR HEARTS EVEN WHEN DISTANCE SEPARATES US"

Mim pulled a handkerchief from her pocket and blew her nose, and she would have said more, but she heard voices at the door which was the gong concluding their time. The key in the lock rattled.

She stepped back and Cratchit stood to his feet with a determined tilt to his chin. She stared at his hand as his fingers tapped on his stick. "WE BOTH GO TO WAR AGAIN / BE SAFE"

* * *

Part 3

The Epilogue: Grandfield Legacy

1919

11

Mim sat in the coal-black shadows of the night garden. She watched as the muted dawn light leaked into the day and faded the deep shadows. Early morning mist cloaked her vision in a comforting shroud. Just to be outside, when she had spent so long inside, felt exposed and vulnerable. Night-time was easier. She would sit and remember the walks she had taken around these grounds as Cratchit was building his stamina. A soldier in training. She slowed her breathing and gripped the arm of the garden bench tightly. For so long she had anticipated what it would be like to walk outside, any time of day, on a whim. It was cruel that circumstances had stolen this joy from her. Just because she hadn't seen active duty, and hadn't travelled to far-flung battle fields, it didn't mean she had not experienced the war. It had come to her, in every traumatised and damaged soldier trying to put his life back together. Yet she was determined to reclaim her comfort of open places; it wasn't easy, and she could only stand it in small doses.

As the morning light leached the shadows away, she retreated to the confines of the small gardening shed that her father used. The Glasshouse had been repossessed by Mrs Whitaker. Evaline Whitaker had emerged from the humiliation of being ousted from her family estate in the name of the war effort, to again reign as queen of the social scene. She had lobbied permission from the curators of the Hospital Board to transform the practical, functional gardening space of the solarium, into a dance hall for fundraising and functions for returned servicemen. Although it was not a ballroom in the manner of her previous life, it was renown as the sparkling jewel of fun and forgetfulness.

Mr Hillman sighed, and his brow furrowed as he watched his

daughter squash herself into a cramped space by a small hatch in the wall that functioned as a window. She closed the shutter against the dawn light. "How are you this morning?" he asked gently.

She didn't answer directly, but sort of shrugged. "I'm still definitely nocturnal. It can't be helped. I will start yapping like a barking owl soon. It will be my second language." She swallowed, and the joke fell flat on her ears. Cratchit had instructed her to tell no one of her knowledge of Morse, and she never had, not even her father. It felt deceptive, to hold a secret that she was already bilingual, but sometimes, as she sat down with a book, she found herself tapping as she read.

Her father maneuvered around the clutter of pots and tools and boxes of catalogued seeds that he had harvested religiously. It annoyed him that he didn't have the space to work efficiently. Just because the armistice had been declared, it hadn't meant less patients or less work. The need to grow produce for Marlie's kitchen was as urgent as ever. He stood an empty wooden fruit box on its end that doubled as a stool and offered it to Mim and then perched himself on another. "Your Mother would be so proud of you. You work so hard, and you have contributed much to help these people. But just because I am proud, it does not stop me being concerned."

She shrugged again. "I'm getting on okay. I read a lot." She looked at her father's brow crease in worry. "Dad, it is better now that I have gone back to simple ward nursing. Ellie has been supportive, and she has given me time to think through various options. I like that I don't have the responsibility of running a ward. I've had plenty of people say it is a backwards step, but being with the patients is what I love. It has been the right decision."

His father sighed. "I had a nurse once who would come to my home on Thredpea Lane. She was very insistent that staying inside and not getting out and about... was not good for me. Made me walk to places that were difficult for me..."

"I'm so sorry Dad. I didn't mean for..."

"I'm not. I am grateful for it." He stood up and stacked up some pots. "And I will offer you the same kindness. But what I ask is also because I need a favour. When they emptied the Glasshouse, they just dumped all the stuff behind the stables, with no regard to my seedlings. I have retrieved what I could, but I've already lost a lot of them, and the others are suffering. I need help to sort it out. I know outside is hard for you during the day, but I was wondering... after your shifts...whether you could..."

"Of course, Dad. Of course. You tell me what you need. Of course." Mim swallowed hard and prayed that being busy would make being outside less of a problem. "I know plenty of the men will be willing to help."

Mim sat down with her father and mapped out a plan that was not just a retrieval plan to save wilting seedling, but a whole restructuring of the nursery. They tossed around what would help make his new-look nursery functional. They ran it past Tibbs, who organised managerial approval. Mim marshalled a group of patients to help sort through the seedling trays and other clutter behind the shed. They were a motley crew, with missing limbs, crutches and bandages, cigarettes, and larrikin jokes. Mr Hillman had been so frustrated as he calculated the loss of his precious seedlings. But he considered the way these young men bore their losses which were far worse than any tray of sprouts, he felt inspired to find a way of making his loss of the greenhouse work out. After all the men were keen and dived in to help make something better.

They took down the fence into the back paddock that had been connected to the stables and used the logs to construct a couple of long walkways along the side boundary. They bordered the path with trestles and criss-crossed wires high over the path so his seedling trays would be shaded by the vines growing along them. It became its own seasonal shade house.

Mim helped plant climbing beans, and choko vines, interspersed with grape vine cuttings. The old horse paddock was now under the care of his crew – patients who had put their name down for gardening duties as part of their rehabilitation. More garden beds were turned so the seedlings would have a home to grow. Part of the plan to continue to supply the kitchen, was that many of the usual vegetables like cucumbers, and melons that sprawled over the ground, were given climbing trestles. He taught the boys how to train them to grow vertically, and others created little string hammocks to support the weight of the fruit. It was a practical solution to make room for more garden beds when space was of a premium.

Mr Hillman watched the men run watering cans made from old billycans punctured with holes along the line of seedling boxes and garden beds, laughing and making jokes. This crew was very different to the one which built Grandfield's fancy glasshouse, but they served well. The construction crew Tibbs had brought in to build the original Glasshouse, had called that vanity project a 'ludicrous gentry folly'. And it was. Foolish to the core. But Hillman realised now, he had not valued the privilege of the convenience of that folly until it was taken away. He was confident this new set-up had the makings of a full-sized market garden that could adequately meet the needs of the hospital kitchen well into the future. His men built a street-stall booth and sold off the extra seasonal produce to the neighbourhood. Tibbs agreed those funds would supplement the maintenance costs of the grounds and garden, and extra was added towards a new shed to house gardening equipment for patients.

* * *

"Mim, I hear the Whitaker's Christmas Gala is on again. This is the first year since the hospital opened, that they are hosting it...early December, like the old days." Mr Hillman sat down at his bench which was now a clear, efficient workspace. Sorting his shed had been the next project that Mr Hillman had asked for Mim's support. She dived into organising the space with such success that one of the men had carved a wooden sign: 'Hillman's Headquarters'. Mim had helped arrange his shelf of reference gardening books, and a filing cabinet of catalogued seeds. A larger shed had been built down behind the stables to accommodate gardening tools, wheelbarrows, and fertilizer bags. Mim regularly brought her Dad a flask of coffee when she visited him between her shifts.

"The Gala? Dad, in all the years I have worked here, I have never gone to *The* Christmas Gala. Why would I start now?"

"It is a new era. Why not put on a pretty dress and have a dance? You deserve to have some fun."

"Fun is sitting in a corner and reading undisturbed."

"Going out might be good for you. What can I do to persuade you?"

"I can't think of anything."

"You know, your mother and I often went dancing. It was a wonderful time in our lives." He came closer, his eyes silently pleaded with her. "Please think about it.

"Okay – I have thought about it. And I am still not going." Mim chuckled and lifted his floppy felt hat, inspecting it carefully. "I have no idea why you have this bee in your bonnet. It's ridiculous."

"Bees! Yes. Hives. We need hives. That is another project that will help the garden and the patients." He jotted a note on a pad on the bench. He looked back at his daughter, shook his head, and his eyes misted with concern. "Mim, helping the men is good for me, but you... you are the most important. Please...I need you to be okay. It doesn't have to be the Gala. They have dances every Friday and Saturday night."

"Which I already know." There was something about his tone. Perhaps it was the reference to her mother that touched her. "Oh, alright... not the Gala though. Pick a Friday night, as those dances are probably smaller. But... I am only going on the condition that you come as my date and let me leave when I have had enough."

"Well, this Friday it is. At least it is a start..."

* * *

Mim danced a waltz with her father as she promised, and waited while he went to get some drinks from the tent pitched outside the Glasshouse for refreshments. These dances were all fundraising events, so even the meagre snacks had a price, unless you were a registered patient. The hospital protocols meant these dances were 'Dry', much to the disgust of Mrs Whitaker who had fond memories of pretty cocktails glasses and fancy punchbowls laced with the finest spirits. Mim shifted the fan around her wrist and huddled back into the corner fanning her face furiously. She glanced at the door as even more soldiers in uniform squeezed into the room, already filled with the constant murmur of superficial conversation and forced laughter buzzing above the music. So much for the Friday night dances being smaller. The gramophone crackled in time with dance steps, blaring out dance tunes.

Mim surveyed the crowd and all she could see was the proliferation of missing limbs, arm-slings, crutches aplenty accompanying the awkward gait of ill-fitting prostheses. And yet they were all having so much fun. These events were another armistice zone. No one would comment or raise eyebrows here. Everyone walked with a limp now, whether external or internal. This was a space dedicated to doing the best that one could with what was left... forgetting and trying to move on. Even moving forward was too ambitious sometimes. Motion, in any form, was the best one could hope for.

Her father returned and handed her a small cup of Marlie's lemonade, and a biscuit – smeared with a little icing in an attempt to make it festive. Mim looked at the offering and raised her eyebrows sceptically. My, how the high-and-mighty Whitaker's had slipped from their branch.

"You look pretty tonight. Why don't you ask someone to dance?" her father suggested with a cheeky grin as he bit into his biscuit.

"Why? You are my date."

He said nothing but surveyed the room with her. He pointed to one man, standing in the opposite corner by a potted plant. He was almost completely obscured by the greenery. "What about him? He looks like he could do with some cheering up." Mim considered him thoughtfully, dressed in an ordinary suit, leaning heavily on a stick. The soldier adjusted his weight and moved awkwardly, suggesting he wore a prosthesis. She decided that helping put someone at ease who was more uncomfortable than herself, was a distraction she could manage. If it would please her father to engage in a dance, and get him off her back, then this target might make her evening mildly worthwhile.

She fixed her eyes on him, and weaved her way along the glass panelled walls that were misted with condensation from the cooler air outside and the warmth of the conversation inside. She wound around the potted plants positioned along the wall, ducking away from couples enthusiastically swinging their dance partners, edging her way towards him.

Finally, she tapped his shoulder. "Excuse me Sir, I was wondering if I could have this dance?"

He turned toward her, and she suppressed a gasp, as his stick came around and bumped her leg. His eyes were sightless, his beard trimmed tidily, his felt hat tilted slightly to the left. A prosthetic leg was not the only matter that would cause him to stay close to the fringes of the crowd.

"I'm sorry, I didn't realise," she hurriedly apologised. "Of course, you may not want to..."

He shrugged noncommittedly. He said nothing.

"We could stay here in the corner. I am not much of a dancer anyway," she said to give him an out, without embarrassment.

He smiled, the line along his lips mildly amused as he nodded.

"My name is Mim... Miriam really," she continued. "I work as a nurse here, but I don't remember meeting you. I have been working here at Grandfield a long time... even before the war."

He paused and his smile broadened as he propped his stick against the wall. He held out his hand. She took it and he firmly drew her into a dance hold.

"Bold," she said, as her head tilted back with a laugh. "I came to dance with you because you seemed a little out of your depth... but I suspect I have read this wrong. You don't seem that uncomfortable with the idea of dancing at all."

"HELLO MIM" He squeezed her hand in a message.

"Oh, my goodness," she exclaimed, "It is you! Yes of course, I recognise your brown suit! I can't believe you still have it." She wrapped her arm around him, almost throwing him off balance with her tight embrace. "You are here! You're okay! I am so glad!" Then after a while she caught herself, stepped back, cleared her throat and allowed him to readjust his posture. He did not let go of her hand.

"YOU WILL HAVE TO LEAD" He squeezed. "I DO NOT SEE"

Mim gasped and smiled in surprise. "IF YOU INSIST" she replied in code as she stepped closer.

"I DO"

They moved in time with the music, stepping in small circles without the flamboyant energetic steps other couples were dancing.

"WHAT IS YOUR NAME" she tapped. "THE WAR IS OVER / YOU CAN TELL ME NOW"

"MAXIMILLIAN CRATCHIT"

Mim shook her head and laughed. "Your name is not really Cratchit," she declared.

"IT IS / ACCORDING TO THE NURSE WHO SAVED MY LIFE"

Mim went silent and studied his face. There were shadows of his familiar gaunt sunken lines that were still shrouded by his beard. She recognised the burn scars puckering along the left side of his face, hidden in part from the tilted brim of his hat. The burns on his neck peeked over the collar of his shirt. She wondered why she had not recognised him. Perhaps it was just that she was not expecting him here. "YOU HAVE ANOTHER NAME"

"I DO" But he made no effort to elaborate.

Had the man with the secrets, completely forgotten his other life, his real identity... or had he reclaimed it? "WHO DO YOU WANT TO BE TONIGHT" she asked.

"NOT VIRTUOUS ENOUGH TO BE KNIGHTLEY" he messaged with a grin. "OBNOXIOUS AND BLIND ENOUGH TO BE ROCHESTER" He tilted his head. "I STILL FEEL THAT STRING / ALTHOUGH IT HAS BEEN STRETCHED BEYOND ENDURANCE"

"Why have you come back?" Mim asked, so completely overcome that she forgot to use code.

"TO CONFIRM SOMETHING"

"WHAT EXACTLY"

"WHETHER YOU REMEMBERED ME"

"YOU ARE NOT EASILY FORGOTTEN SIR"

"NOR YOU"

They danced close. Mim sighed. Things suddenly seemed okay with the world... even after everything. The music stopped and their steps paused.

"DO YOU WANT TO GET OUT OF HERE / GO FOR A WALK"

"OH YES PLEASE"

They walked around the grounds. Following the paths through the grounds. It was a relief to get away from the people and the noise.

"COME TO THE GALA / BE MY DATE"

"SORRY I DON'T DO GALAS"

"WHY NOT"

How could she explain? She couldn't really. Mostly, it was that Christmas could not to be reduced to an extravagant party and dance music.

But it also had memories of a nursery and a little girl... and a brother with a book. She shrugged. "TOO MANY PEOPLE" That was also true.

"NEW YEARS THEN" he tapped.

"That is over a month away! Surely, I can see you before then?" she stammered in shock.

He smiled as if that was the funniest thing he had heard. "WE HAVENT SEEN EACH OTHER FOR 2 YEARS"

"LONGER ACTUALLY / I MISSED YOU EVERY DAY" She looked across at his profile in the dark and wondered if she had been too bold.

He smiled and straightened up as if something was resolved for him. "ME TOO / NEW YEARS IS PERFECT / I HAVE BUSINESS TO ATTEND TO / IT WILL TAKE SOME TIME TO SORT OUT"

"DO YOU HAVE THE HELP YOU NEED"

"MY SISTER"

"Oh."

"PROMISE ME YOU WILL BE MY DATE"

"For New Years?" She hesitated, and then quickly responded. She didn't want him to get the idea that she didn't want to go out with him. She had been honest about not being a fan of large numbers of people in such a closed space. "OF COURSE".

He nodded again. "YOU DO ME GOOD MIM HILLMAN"

She held his hand... transfusing hope back through her veins. not wanting to let him go.

"COMING BACK WAS HARD / IT SHOCKED ME WHAT IT WAS LIKE HERE WITHOUT YOU" His hand trembled.

"I AM HERE NOW"

"NEW YEARS EVE / DONT FORGET" There was an urgency in the way he tapped, stumbling over his words.

"IMPOSSIBLE," Mim tapped back, and then she leant in to reassure him and whispered, "I know what you look like now Mr Cratchit, even though you are changed, you are still the same. I will be here. Don't *you* forget."

He sighed; relief and reassurance in his breath, and he nodded gallantly, "NOT A CHANCE" They walked back towards the Glasshouse where he would meetup with his ride, their silence mixed with so many unspoken questions. What had happened in the time that had passed? Could they really pick up where they left off? Mim thought it was strange that he bypassed her hints that she would willingly assist with his care. They quietly made their way towards the crowd of people saying their goodbyes as the bright lights of the Glasshouse spilt over onto the driveway; the brash notes of jazz music still blaring. Closing these dances in time to meet the curfew, was always a challenge.

"THANK YOU FOR COMING MIM / TIL NEW YEARS THEN"

She left him standing by a potted shrub near the door and retreated into the darkness and the quietness of the garden again. The questions kept coming in tears of quiet gratitude and relief, as she sat listening to the owls and curlews for a long time, and eventually she returned to her quarters.

* * *

13

Mim could think of nothing else. Maximillian Cratchit was alive! She had tried to find him, but she had no information to go on apart from Case File 7285. That got her nowhere. The clerk shook his head sympathetically and mumbled something about "Classified", and M.I.A. She had even tried to follow up with Dr Redmond, but he was locked away in his family's mansion not taking visitors. None of that mattered now. He was no longer missing in action. He had not just survived, but more importantly he had remembered her. That string had drawn them back together. He said she had saved his life. He had danced with her. He had asked her to be his date. A real date... and this time she did feel that flutter of anticipation as she thought about his invitation. Actually, not a flutter... sometimes that feeling was so overwhelming the nausea hit her until she would puke.

Over the next few days Mim reviewed every interaction she had with Maximillian with meticulous attention. From the moment the doctor had allocated her duties for this strange man with secrets, to a chance encounter at a Friday night dance. She thought about Maximillian's insistence that she learn Morse Code. Military intel aside, she could finally acknowledge all the frustration she endured to learn was worth it. What a privilege to have all those uninterrupted conversations in the seclusion of a hospital isolation ward or walking through the night garden. It gave them privacy even when immersed in the raucous atmosphere of the dance hall where speaking people had to shout to be heard.

Mim realised at the dance she barely noticed Maximillian's scars, which was so different to when she was nursing him. Back then she was constantly inspecting, applying cream, gently massaging, trying to stretch the new tender skin to minimize those puckering scars. Every time she tended a patient, she reminded herself, that just like Cratchit, he had lived a life before this. A life before the war. A life before pain and injury. That was the person she was nursing back to health. As she relived that dance over and over, she could feel the familiarity of him: the way he held her as they moved; the way he smiled as he tapped; the way he convinced her to be his date. She could tell he had once been a very confident man... perhaps the rank of army... and that sureness was coming back.

Her father's insistence that she wear a pretty dress to the dance was a funny, useless detail when the only person she had danced with was blind. It was one advantage his lack of sight offered, because she really didn't own a pretty dress. Not anymore. What she had noticed though, was what it was like to dance... and to feel him close... and to notice the heat that flushed her cheeks; perhaps from the crowded room... perhaps not. She remembered that same warmth on her skin as they walked around the garden in the cool breeze of night.

As she counted off the days until the New Year, she kept her encounter with Mr Cratchit close to her heart. She quietly celebrated Christmas by sharing a piece of Marlie's Christmas cake and a glass of lemonade with her father in the garden. The cake was scattered with sultana's, rather than the rich dark fruit cake they used to have, but this Christmas, at least they *had* cake. It reminded her how Christmas celebrated a message of restoration from pain and chaos: that was always God's plan. Maximillian coming home was surely a sign of restoration in her life. She hoped so. She was relieved that he was no longer patient case file 7285, and she didn't need to feel conflicted about whether loving him was appropriate or not.

Yes, the New Year's Eve Party was a date. A true date. The anticipation that pounded her heart was exhilarating... and she did want to wear a pretty dress. Even if Maximillian could not see, she wanted to know that when she danced with him, she felt beautiful. This was important to her. She really wanted to get it right. She went to her cupboard and inspected her few ordinary dresses that now looked even shabbier than before. She had lived so long in a nurse's uniform that she had forgotten what wearing a good going-out dress was like. All those years, hiding books within the covers of women's fashion magazines, and she couldn't remember one article that could possibly help her in this moment.

The weeks that she thought would go on forever while she waited for the New Year to come, were quickly going by and she had found no solution. There was only one person that she could think of who would be able to help her with this... and it was an embarrassing concession to make. Anna. Anna Whitaker.

Since the Christmas Gala, there was a huge buzz about the return of Anna to Grandfield. She had grown up. She had served her country. But now she was back, engaged to Rick Barnes – Tibby and Marlie's son. Mim never considered that she had been friends with Anna, but she hoped that there might be enough connection from those years in the nursery that would permit her to receive this request favourably. Mim spoke with Marlie, who directed her to their quarters where Anna was staying. Mim tentatively tapped on the door.

"Coming!" was the cheery call from inside. When the door opened Anna looked at her blankly with a frown. Then she burst into a glorious smile. "Hillman! Oh, how wonderful to see you! Come in. Come in."

Mim nodded and followed her into the sitting-room. "Hello Anna," she said tentatively.

"Well, it is a long time since you were supervising ladders in my stockings! Oh, it is good to see you Hillman."

"Anna, I would like it if you could call me Mim."

"Of course. Mim. I'm sorry. It is a bit of a habit I suppose... inground by years of tradition. You are right, surnames are such an impersonal form or address. How are you? I hear you are the hero of nursing in this hospital."

"No more than anyone else. We all do our part. And you... I hear congratulations are in order. I wish you well."

"Oh well... you know me. I spent my childhood chasing Rick up trees. Guess I caught up with him finally."

Mim smiled. "I wish you every happiness. What are you doing now... other than getting ready for a wedding?"

"Well, not nursing, that is for certain. That wasn't for me. Rick is helping me embark on a little enterprise, developing a skin lotion that I am hoping the patients may find helpful. It is based on an old recipe of Marlie's mother, that really helped heal my hands."

Mim gasped. "The stink ointment!"

Anna looked at her curiously. "You know this?"

"Yes! Marlie gave me a sample to try on a burn's patient. It worked wonderfully! Although I suspect the patient's sheets still reek of it. I think I used buckets of the stuff. I was amazed she was able to get the ingredients, but very grateful she could still make it up." Very grateful. This had significantly helped Cratchet's recovery.

"That is a wonderful endorsement. My project is trying to find a way to mask the smell but still keep the healing qualities of the cream." Anna showed her the scars on her hands, and the progress of the samples. She urged her to try a couple of variations, rubbing them gently into her skin.

"I like the jasmine. It is very fragrant at night," Mim said. Yes, still nocturnal.

"Would you be interested in using this with some of your other patients, just to get their feedback? The men are probably not going to like the floral scents very much, so I am trying other blends that are more masculine, like citrus, or sandalwood, or pine." She offered her to smell some oils that she had.

Mim smiled. Sandalwood. That would suit Mr Cratchit very well. "This reminds me of your enterprising days with the street-stand selling lemonade and berries. My father has taken a leaf out of your book with his own stall to sell surplus produce from the garden. But not just mulberries now, there are a whole range of seasonal options. The men have built the shed down behind the stables from those funds."

Anna smiled, with an echo of sadness. "Those stalls remind me of Chrissy. I am calling this range of lotions, '*Chrystal's Balm*' – at least the floral ones anyway. I will probably need a companion name for the others. Chrissy's birthday was in spring, and we shared a matching set of crystal dishes like the ones that will carry the lotion."

"Oh Anna, I think this is a beautiful tribute to your friend. The friendship you had with Chrissy was uniquely special."

"Thanks, Mim. I appreciate that."

"Anna, I wanted to ask a favour... I wondered if you could help me with something."

"Well, sure. If I can..."

"I have a date for the New Year's Eve Party..."

Anna face lit up with the intrigue. "A date? That sounds exciting..." Anna gave no indication that she knew anything about this particular invitation. For Anna, silence was as natural as breathing. She understood what it meant to be exposed as a Whitaker.

"Oh yes, it is wonderful! But I have been in a Nurses' uniform so long, I have forgotten what good fashion looks like. I wondered if you could give me some ideas."

"Oh rubbish. I can do better than ideas. Since the Gala, Mother has been determined that my wardrobe be updated. I know what you mean about the nurses' uniforms, but honestly, I've been overwhelmed by the fashion. You can borrow one of my dresses."

"Really? I hadn't meant to suggest that."

"Oh come. I can't wear more than one dress at a time anyway. You spent years making sure my hems, bows and hats were immaculate. Now it is my turn."

"Ahh, yes. There was always a matching hat," Mim chuckled.

"Let me do this as a favour to you." Anna went across to her room and opened the wardrobe. "See, Mother is determined that I represent the Whitaker name in a suitable gown and hat."

Mim gasped at the array of beautiful dresses that hung there. The Anna of options still existed. "Anna these are beautiful."

She giggled... echoes of a little girl from a far-away time. "Mrs Hargrave is delighted to have a side-line that does not involve starched uniforms and linen."

"She is such a master. Which one will you be wearing?"

"I'm not sure, but I was tending towards this ice blue one with the silver beading. The tassels are cute."

"That will look so beautiful on you." Mim sighed and sobered. "Actually Anna, to be honest the dress can be plain. My date is... well, of humble circumstances, and he cannot see. His eyes were injured."

"Plain? Oh no. Humble or not, a man likes his girl to be smashing. And if he cannot see, it just means that the colour is not important... but it has to *feel* perfect. Here. Close your eyes." Anna directed Mim to stand before the wardrobe and guided her hand along the row of dresses. Then she pulled a scarf from her cupboard and wrapped it around Mim's eyes in a blindfold. "Now tell me what feels good." Mims fingers travelled along the hangers and lingered on one dress. Anna took it and placed it on her bed. "Any others?" A couple of other dresses came out. "Okay. Now we try them on. No. Don't take the scarf off. Not yet. You are going to feel like the prettiest date at the dance."

Mim slipped into the dress at the top of the pile. She shimmied and bobbed. The fabric felt wonderful, and the beading was intricate. She ran her fingers over the beaded patterns. "You know. I think I like the idea of no beading... just the feeling of smooth fabric."

"Okay... don't make any decisions yet. But try this one on... it has less beading, but lots of tassels. I like the way they swish on my legs."

Mim laughed. She felt like the spoilt daughter of a Whitaker as she slipped it on. She swayed. "They do swish," she said with a smile. "That feels so lovely." But as she ran her hands over the tucks across her hips, she was less certain.

She tried on a couple more and Anna encouraged her to give each dress an appraisal. "Now try this one," said Anna with an air that she held the trump card in her hand.

"Oh yes!" said Mim without hesitation. "This is it. This feels absolutely perfect." It was made with a light silk-velvet with a chiffon overlay on the drop-waisted skirt.

"Are you sure?" Anna asked.

"Perfectly!"

"No doubts?"

"None."

"Okay then." Anna positioned her in front of the mirror, selected a matching headpiece, applied a little bit a lip balm. "I agree. You have good taste Mim. This is the dress for a New Year's Eve party that will knock out your date." She gently removed the blindfold.

Mim gasped. The dress was a pale apricot, that shimmered and danced around her in a veil of loveliness. "Oh Anna, this is too beautiful. Perhaps not."

"Perhaps definitely. Consider it compensation for all the hours you struggled to have me looking presentable when I refused to come down out of the trees. I insist."

* * *

14

Mim looked in the mirror again and hardly knew what to think. She had never thought of apricot as her colour, but it shimmered so beautifully and danced off the lights reflecting in her dark hair. She could even imagine herself on the cover of one of those magazines. If Maximillian Cratchit could see, he would hardly recognise her. But he had never seen her, and he had nothing to compare this to. Mim felt a pang of disappointment at that thought. However, she anticipated his arms holding her around the soft fabric of her dress as they danced; his hand squeezing her name into her palm as they moved; his smile as he felt her close; his breath on her cheek. The hope for these moments were enough to propel her forward through her shyness and her dread of the crowded dance hall. She made her way down the stairs, across the verandah, she paused before she launched herself out onto the lawn and across to the Glasshouse. The lights were too bright, the music was too loud, the dancing too frenzied, the laughing too forced, as partygoers foxtrotted on the lawn in groups that spilt over into tennis court.

Mim took a deep breath to settle her anxiety and ignored their exuberance. She was focused on the back corner of the Glasshouse. If only she had arranged to meet in the garden, in the dark, away from all this noise. But he had asked her to come. "Don't forget", he had said. As if she could forget! He had even sent her a note in his scratched hand, crooked on the plain paper, confirming their date. There was no return address. Remembering was not her problem. Perhaps she should try to forget. The whole world, it seems, was ushering in the new decade with a determination to anesthetise their memories. But there was a sober light in her eyes as she made her way to the door. A war could not be forgotten with bright lights and loud music. The noise would never be loud enough. Not really.

She walked around the glass walls of the solarium, ducking the lively swinging arms of the dancers. Maybe some time in the future, she would want to dance with that kind of energy. In truth, a gentle waltz with a man who limped was more her style. She looked over at the far corner and swallowed her disappointment. It was still empty... there was no brown suit waiting for her. A few couples huddled there, catching their breath by an open window, fanning their faces.

She made her way around the walls of the Glasshouse, to the far corner, just as she had promised. She wasn't standing by the pot plant long, when she heard a ripple of whispers, like a tidal surge, run across the room. The heir of Grandfield had come home. He had served his country; he was a captain in the army; he deserved the honours bestowed on him. This year he had bypassed tradition and chosen the New Year's Party, not the Christmas Gala, for the annual Whitaker address. He was going to announce his plans for Grandfield. Mim shook her head with a frown. Everyone knew Max Whitaker didn't stay for New Years. Who cared if his routine had been thrown out by a war? Get in line Mr Whitaker. She had met Maxwell Whitaker, and she was pretty sure a Federal Government held more sway than whatever grand plans he might have to reclaim Grandfield as his family inheritance. The community still needed a hospital. They had too many patients who would struggle to find a placement elsewhere without this facility.

Suddenly the music stopped. Mim turned to see the Whitaker family walk through the door. As they stepped through the dancers, the people parted like Moses crossing the Red Sea. Anna looked gorgeous in her ice-blue beaded frock, walking on the arm of Rick Barnes. Mr Whitaker Senior was not present – he rarely left the Stablemaster's house now. Mrs Whitaker held the elbow of a tall man which Mim assumed was her son, Max Whitaker. He had changed some from the socialite who had dallied in the nursery one Christmas Gala night: his hair was cut military short; his clean-shaven face bore scars that he wore with that same Whitaker confidence as his felt hat that sat on his head with a tilt. He too walked with a limp, but Max still dressed well. He wore a handsome dark grey suit, smart and distinguished. He sported a gold chain across his vest pocket, and his stiff white collar and bold necktie was tied in a fashionable Windsor knot. He looked straight ahead and was unmoved by the smiles and flashy waves from the ladies as he passed. Another young man followed in their wake, carrying a leather satchel, with papers poking out the top. He wore an old-fashioned pinstripe navy suit that was a too big for him. He looked flustered and adjusted his glasses nervously as he stayed close to their party. They went straight to the centre of the back wall of the Glasshouse where a small platform and podium was set up. Mrs Whitaker stepped forward, and with skilful command of the crowd, she hushed the whispers and said her farewells to 1919. She introduced her son Max and asked him to say a few words.

Anna and her brother walked forward together to the podium. All those years ago, Anna was right. Max was still the favourite. The crowd applauded as the grey suit acknowledged them with a wave. The young pin-striped man shuffled forward and stuffed a paper into Anna's hand.

The applause settled as she smoothed out the wrinkles on the sheet and she started to read with a loud voice. "Ladies and gentlemen. On behalf of my brother and myself, it is our pleasure to usher in a new decade with you. May 1920 be blessed with a restoration of every happiness. We are honoured to share this moment with you here at Grandfield..." There was a wave of applause deafening as it reverberated around the Glasshouse. Huh. Max had said Grandfield was outdated. He had been right on that point. Very outdated. Yet here he was, playing to the crowd, enjoying the limelight. He didn't seem at all uncomfortable as the masses before him clapped. There was something endearing about royalty coming out to join the masses, all be it, a self-made aristocracy reigning over a mere local neighbourhood serfdom. She thought it was odd that Max said nothing at all. Like Moses, who needed Aaron to speak on his behalf, Anna was the family mouthpiece on this occasion. It was a sign of ushering in a new generation, her mother passing the baton for her to be given that privilege. Anna held herself well. She was, after all, her mother's daughter.

Anna continued. "I know there has been a lot of speculation about the future of the hospital. This New Year, the hospital will return under the custodianship of The Whitaker Foundation. My brother and I want to assure you that the hospital will stay fully operational. No jobs will be lost. You have our commitment, that as we sit on the Board together, we will safeguard the legacy given by the men and women, who have served our country; often at great personal cost and sacrifice. Nothing will jeopardise the care that our men and women deserve after serving their country so gallantly."

Huh. Anna was taking her place in business after all, not just her entrepreneurial project with lotions, but sitting beside her brother in governing this kingdom. Mim smiled as she watched Anna confidently step into this new role and felt a warmth of satisfaction that, in some unseen way, as one of the Grandfield servants, she had contributed to its grand heritage.

Mim didn't really take too much notice of what was said after that. Once she heard the news that her job was secure, she went back to scanning the crowd for that familiar brown suit. She craned her neck to look around the heads of people listening intently to the official announcement. A burst of applause and cheers drew her attention back to the front podium as Mrs

Whitaker stood up again and regally commanded the masses to welcome in a new decade with fun and frivolity. There was another cheer as the air was filled with colourful streamers and with an enthusiastic hip-hip-hooray the official proceedings were complete. The music and dancing resumed.

A voice behind her spoke. "Excuse me Miss Hillman. Mr Whitaker was wondering if he could have this dance."

Mim turned around quickly to the face of the young man, dressed in pinstriped navy, who had handed Anna the speech. Like so many young men, his eyes disclosed he had seen too much. He swiped at a streamer that draped across his shoulder. "Oh, I'm sorry. I am expecting someone else, and I am here waiting for him." She nodded quickly and went back to scanning the dancers. "Please pass on my apologies," she said simply, looking around the room. *Had he forgotten? Had he been delayed? Was he coming?*

"Miss Hillman, he really does insist," the young man said officially.

Mim turned towards the grey suit, and nodded, "Your insistence is of no consequ..." and any further sound died on her lips.

She suddenly realised his eyes were sightless. She could see his cufflinks, under the sleeves of his grey suit, the same cufflinks he wore a decade ago, now glinting as his hand rested on the young man's shoulder, tapping out a message. "I WILL TAKE IT FROM HERE" He reached out his hand, and Mim stared at it dumbfounded. Finally, she took his hand. "I AM HERE," he pressed into her palm.

"You? You are Maximillian Cratchit?" His face, now clean shaven, did match what she knew of Cratchit. His eyes, although obviously could not see... were recognisable, even though they were no longer that startling cufflink Whitaker blue. But the clothes, and the name, and the rank of captain that everyone talked about... She shook her head, dazed.

"GOOD EVENING MIM / I AM YOUR DATE" he tapped. "I AM GLAD YOU CAME" There were hints of a familiar smile on his lips. Pleased and confident. And Mim, in that moment, could not tell where she remembered it from. Was it Cratchit or Max who lounged comfortably in the Nursery?

"No! No. You can't be. I have waited all this time for Maximillian. We had a string! He promised he would be here. He promised me a dance. You can't be him!"

"MIM / LET ME EX..."

She stared at him in shock, pulled away before he could finish. "No, I don't believe it!" And she pushed through the crowd and fled out into the darkness.

* * *

Mim went back to work. It was another death, another aspect of profound loss that this war had inflicted. Why couldn't she be happy that Cratchit turned out to be the rich heir, the crown prince, the obnoxious Rochester. But she couldn't. She missed Maximillian. He was the one who loved her. And she had loved him. Deeply. She realised that now. All those months, where they had lived and worked together in the confines of one room, had formed into years since he had last pressed her hand in farewell. He was the one she had kept the fireside fires burning for, until he could come home. She had been loyal to *Cratchit*. She wasn't swapping him out for a flashy suit and a title. She was faithful to the man without rank who had been isolated and alone, holding secrets that could cost him his life; it was a risk to love someone like that. Not someone with a whole estate to his name, with people under his hire. Mim sighed as she signed off the last of her charts and filed it on the shelf at the nurses' station. She spoke again to the night nurse coming on shift, giving her a quick update of the patient in bed six who had spiked a fever. Then she reported to the Ward Sister as she was leaving. "Good night, Ellie," she said as she put her nurse's cape around her shoulders.

"Mim, are you okay?" Ellie was not just her supervising Sister. They had worked together for many years. They were friends.

Mim nodded and shrugged. "Tired. That's all. It's been a big day."

"Well okay. Thanks for your help today." She paused. "Mim, if you need to talk.... I'm here. You know that right?"

Mim nodded and stepped out into the night. It was a relief to a walk around the grounds in the dark again. The summer night air was warm, and she stayed close to the shadows as she walked. When someone passed by, she plunged into the deep pockets of darkness in the garden to avoid detection. A few nurses walked the paths, taking a stroll before going back to their quarters after their shift. Their chatter faded and the silence was restored. Mim emerged from the shadows and sat down on a bench seat. The birds were quiet tonight, but the crickets and cicadas merged loudly with her thoughts.

Mim gasped as she remembered that Cratchit had told her that he had a sister who supported him. Anna! His sister is Anna! Even as Anna helped Mim with her dress, all smiles and obliging generosity, she knew about this date. Anna was again that spoilt precocious eleven-year-old Miss, playacting in cahoots with her brother at her expense.

Yes, she had been played the fool. Completely.

* * *

15

"Mim, are you okay?" Her father asked that same question Ellie offered. He handed her a drink of water in an enamel mug as she sat in his office. The wooden fruit boxes had been replaced with wooden chairs, sturdy and functional.

Mim silently shook her head, her teeth gritted. "Mostly I am just mad. I am so angry. He had no right!"

Her father drank from his mug and said nothing.

"Did you know Dad? Did you know it was him?" Mim stared at the speckles on the enamel mug. Lapis blue. Whitaker blue. It looked like the night sky studded with stars. More reminders merging in a confusing mess.

"Whitaker came to see me. He had that young man with him... in the suit, and it took me a while to join the dots, but he explained it... you know, using the kid as a translator. He asked if he could date my daughter."

"Oh no, Dad. Not you too! Why didn't you tell me? Why wouldn't you let me know."

"He wanted me to convince you to go to the Christmas Gala. That's all. And when you wouldn't, it seemed innocent enough to try for a Friday Night dance. You needed to get out... that's why I went along with it. But after that, my part was done."

"Done! You shoved him in my face!"

"I made a suggestion, that's all... and you followed it up on your own volition."

"It sounds all so innocuous, but this was a conspiracy in league of a global world war. Is that why you wouldn't come to the New Year's Eve Dance?"

"I didn't go to that dance because I'm too old for all that noise and carry on, just to stay up late, to be tired the next day. I have a job that doesn't go away just because a new calendar flips its page. Besides, you had your date, and I didn't think you would need me."

"I do need you. You're supposed to be the one person who has my back!"

He took off his hat and scratched his head. "Mim, I have your back. Always. I do. But I could see he was struggling. He reminded me of how I was when your mother died. I know what it is like to lose the one you love. And how you were after that Friday night dance... I could tell that you liked him deeply. You are a discerning young woman Mim. I keep reminding myself that Max is not his father. He insisted on meeting you and disclosing this his own way. I didn't agree with all of it, and I urged him to tell you up front. I suppose he thought it would be a grand surprise."

"Well, it was that... although I wouldn't call it grand."

Her father took another drink. "Mim, you need to talk with Anna..."

"Absolutely not. She was in on the whole thing as well."

"She's not a wilful kid anymore Mim. She came to see me when she couldn't find you. She was quite distraught that you were so upset."

Mim shook her head and sighed. "Well okay. I do need to return the dress anyway."

* * *

Mim knocked quietly on the door. She waited a moment, hung the dress in its cover over a hook by the door and turned to go. There, she had tried. She heard the door open and when she turned around Anna was there. "Mim! Thank you for coming. Please. Come in."

"I won't stay. I just came to return the dress." She picked it up off the hook and passed it over, but Anna didn't take it. She stepped aside and opened the door wider. "Please come in. I want to apologise."

The line of Mim's mouth was firm as she stepped through the door. Anna took a deep breath. "Mim, I am so sorry..."

Mim nodded curtly, draped the dress over the chair and went to leave.

Anna stepped forward, tears in her eyes. "Mim please. Keep the dress. It suits you."

"I doubt I could wear it again. It is not quite my style after all."

"Mim, I meant no disrespect, but Max... the idea of connecting with you again... that meant the world to him. I thought it was strange to start with, but it became clear that finding you was the one thing that was holding him together. I didn't know you were his nurse. I didn't even know he was here at Grandfield during the war, but I am so very grateful that he had family looking after him. You saved his life Mim, he is very clear about that. But it was not just his body you saved... it was his whole self. You kept him sane. He said he went back to his post because he needed to close off that part of his life and leave it behind, so he could be with you free and clear. You helped him close that book. Not just a chapter... but the whole horror story. You must know, he did it because of you Mim. He would not be here now, taking on these responsibilities without you and what you mean to him."

Mim stood there, unmoved. "I think I would prefer to hear this from him."

"Oh, he will tell you. I know he will. I really just want you to let him do that. Please. Hear what he has to say. He loves you Mim. He does. And I know, by the way you wore that dress, you love him too."

Mim stared at her and shook her head. "No, you are wrong. I never loved your brother, I loved someone else completely different." She turned on her heel, and walked through the door, and left it open.

* * *

"Sister Hillman?"

"Yes?" Mim looked up from the bed she was making. "Oh. It's you."

"Yes Ma'am." The man in the pinstriped suit shuffled uncomfortably.

"Well? What is it that you want?"

"Ma'am, Capt... Mr Whitaker wanted me to tell you that he requires you come to his office to see him."

Mim was unimpressed. She raised her brow. "He *requires* it? Does he now?'

"Yes, Ma'am."

"Well, you can tell *Mister* Whitaker that the hospital administrator, and the nursing staff have no bearing on each other. I am not required to meet with him, and he cannot summon me."

The Pinstripe looked panicked as he fiddled with his spectacle frames. "Oh Ma'am, please. Please just come."

"No! I have no obligation at all to attend his office. My job is here with the patients."

"But..."

"No."

"Very well Ma'am. If you change your mind, Mr Whitaker will see you at any time."

"Don't disturb yourself. I won't."

Every day, the Pinstripe came to the ward, and made the same request. Every day she declined.

Ellie, the Ward Sister spoke to her about it.

Her father spoke to her about it.

Marlie spoke to her about it.

Anna spoke to her about it... again.

Even Tibbs had something to say.

Stoically Mim made her way to his office, just so she could finally close the topic. The young man in the navy pinstripe, sat behind a desk by the door. He stood up when he saw her, clutching the edge of his desk like it was his lifeline. A look of clear relief infused his eyes, made larger by his glasses. "You are here to see Mr Whitaker?"

"Yes. You know that I am. You have been harassing me for a fortnight about the fact he wants to see me. I am here because I have been summoned." It was humiliating to acknowledge it took so little time for her to relent. Just two weeks. But this wasn't going away. She might as well get it over with.

"Take a seat Ma'am." Mim rolled her eyes and stood still. Of all the palaver! Was this the way it would be now? Yes Sir; no Ma'am; three bags full... all that high-brow carryon...

The man rapped on the door. To some it might have sounded like an extended creative knock. "SHES HERE" There was a pause before the door opened, and Rick Barnes excused himself and left. He was working as the hospital accountant. Mim stood in the doorway for a moment. This was the same room that had been their hospital room for months. Instead of featuring a hospital bed, there were two large office desks, exactly the same. Max inhabited one, and the other was set to the side, filled with files, ledgers and books which presumably were used by Rick in his administrative duties. There was a chesterfield lounge, and a deep, winged reading chair, that once inhabited the library, was positioned by the window overlooking the courtyard. "Miss Hillman to see you, Sir," said the Suit. Max sat at his desk and nodded. "This way Ma'am," the man said as he ushered her inside.

"THANK YOU PHILIP / YOU MAY GO" Max used a clicker beside him that emitted short and long tones. Philip closed the door behind him as he left.

Mim shook her head and raised an eyebrow. "So now you have a puppy?"

He shrugged. "HE IS MY ASSISTANT / MANAGES MY DIARY / READS REPORTS TO ME / TAKES DICTATION"

"That sounds efficient."

"EFFICIENT WOULD BE DOING THOSE THINGS MYSELF / WE MANAGE"

"He's a nervous little pup. He looks like he could pee on the carpet at any moment."

"HES FINDING HIS FEET / DOES A GOOD JOB"

There was an extended pause. "Why am I here?" she asked eventually.

"I WANTED TO TALK"

"I seriously doubt there is much to say."

"WHY ARE YOU UPSET"

"Do you genuinely have no idea?" He said nothing but waited. "Damn it Max, it is pretty obvious! You lied to me!"

"I NEVER LIED"

"Semantics! This whole time, you were posing as someone you were not! How can I believe you?"

"APART FROM SECURITY PROTOCOLS THAT BOUND MY DISCLOSURES I LIKED BEING WHO YOU WANTED ME TO BE"

"I wanted to know *you*... not just some idea of you! How can you judge me for that?"

"IM NOT THE ONE JUDGING HERE"

"But I don't even know who you are. It is impossible to work out which version of you I am supposed to like."

"SO WITH ALL YOUR INVESTIGATING YOU STILL DON'T KNOW"

"What investigating?"

"IN THE NURSERY YEARS AGO / YOU SAID I WAS AN ENIGMA / YOU WERE GOING TO INVESTIGATE"

She sat down on a chair and shook her head, defeated. "Max, how can I investigate when I didn't even know who was in front of me? You hog-tied me, and I feel stupid. You were playing with my heart, and I fell for you hard, but I didn't even know it. None of this was fair."

"NOT ONCE WAS I PLAYING"

"If I had known who you were, I would have had a chance to be more guarded. Keep my distance. You didn't even give me that opportunity."

"EXACTLY"

She looked at him sitting behind the desk, his suit and tie immaculate, echoes of a young man in the library... or the man in the nursery off to play the favourite son at the Christmas Gala. Which part was the man, with his shoes kicked off, his tie undone, talking about books? Which part was Cratchit, the rankless custodian of war intelligence, teaching her Morse with more skill and enthusiasm than Anna's childhood tutor, Mr Meade, ever showed? "Max, what I had with Cratchit, is very different to what is possible with you."

"WHY / WE ARE THE SAME PERSON"

"But that is just it. You are not! You are Max Whitaker."

"I AM"

"You are a ranking officer! A captain no less!"

"I WAS"

"You own a private hospital!"

"I AM THE CHAIRMAN AT LEAST"

She sighed. This was never going to work. Her voice faded. "See! You *really* don't get it!"

"TELL ME / WHY DID YOU CALL ME CRATCHIT"

"You know why. That book you gave me... A Christmas Carol... it was such a generous, spontaneous gift, and Dickens is a master. Cratchit is the unsung hero."

He nodded. "SO IT IS NOT JUST THE BOOK / THE GIFT AND THE GIVER ARE CONNECTED"

"Regardless of how I came by it, it is a story that I love. Cratchit was poor and loyal – qualities that persisted through hardship."

"DID YOU LOVE THIS CRATCHIT"

"You know I did. So much. So very much."

"BUT IT WAS NOT JUST A CHARACTER FROM THE BOOK THAT YOU LOVED BUT YOUR PATIENT"

"Oh, how I miss him. When I thought I had him back it was a dream come true. But you, Max Whitaker, you have taken him away forever. And I'm not sure I can forgive you for that."

"WHAT IF THERE WAS A WAY YOU COULD HAVE CRATCHIT BACK"

She frowned. "But there isn't. He isn't even real. I made him up."

"YOU MADE UP HIS NAME / EVERYTHING ELSE WAS REAL"

"I was nursing a cot-case soldier who had no value outside the secrets he held."

"TRUE / BUT THAT WAS NOT JUST CRATCHIT / THAT WAS ME"

"I was nursing Case File 7285 who lost his leg and nearly his life."

"TRUE / BUT THAT WAS NOT JUST CRATCHIT / THAT WAS ME"

"I fell in love with a man who would wake me up in the middle of the night to go walking in the dark so we could talk for hours."

"THAT WAS NOT JUST CRATCHIT / THAT WAS ME"

"It can't be both. You are not him!" She stamped her foot and rubbed her palm across her forehead in frustration. He was not getting this.

"MIM" He stood up and ran his hand along the side of the desk as he walked towards her voice. He faulted. His prosthesis knocked the side of the desk and he stumbled. Her nursing instinct had her there beside him in a moment to support him from falling. He reached for her hand automatically, as they had done a thousand times in the dark. He held her tightly, as he stabilised himself and regained his balance. "MIM": two dashes; two dots; two dashes. She closed her eyes and felt his hand in hers, as she led him to the lounge. They sat there, still and silent, for a long time. The string tightened, rib to rib, and it was drawing her in.

"MIM / IT IS ME"

She sat beside him holding his hand as naturally as if the years had not passed by at all. Mim could feel his blood transfusing her body, strengthening, fortifying, reassuring. Suddenly they were back by the bed: practicing walking; disagreeing about the books they read; floundering around the rhythm of morse; gridlocked in silence; grading Marlie's soups.

"MIM PLEASE DONT JUDGE THIS BOOK BY ITS COVER / INSIDE IT IS STILL ME"

More silence.

"IT IS YOU" she finally conceded. Tears welled in her eyes as she felt her heart reviving. "IT IS YOU." She threw her arms around him in a tight embrace. "Oh Maximillian, I have missed you so much!"

His arms drew her close in a moment and he held her with relief. His hand on her back gently tapped a message. "WE CAN GET THROUGH THE REST BECAUSE WE HAVE ALREADY SURMOUNTED THE WORST"

* * *

"SO MIM I HEAR YOU HAVE THIS AMAZING DRESS THAT DESERVES A DANCE"

"ITS NOT MINE" She shook her head. "Which is something that you also know. It is Anna's dress."

"YOU OWE ME A DANCE / YOU BALED ON OUR DATE"

"You cannot hold me to that! I was side-swiped!"

"TOMORROW NIGHT / COME DRESSED FOR A DATE"

"I really don't want to do the Glasshouse. I am not up for crowds and loud." She felt kind of pleased with herself that she could be honest. Honest was better. She demanded it of him, but she was aware that she needed to try harder as well.

Max shrugged. "OK / NO GLASSHOUSE / TOMORROW NIGHT / DONT FORGET"

"That terrifies me. Last time I had a date with you, it nearly ripped out my heart."

"COME TO THE OFFICE / 2200 / DRESS FOR YOUR DATE"

* * *

Mim tapped on the office door. "IM HERE" She ran her hands down her dress, soft and shimmery. She felt her heart quicken. Was it fear, or anticipation?

She heard the clicks come from the office in reply, "COME IN" She opened the door and stepped inside. Max was standing behind his desk, his hand on his clicker. The room was lit only by the dim glow of a small hurricane lamp, not unlike the one she used to take on their walks. He wore Maximillian Cratchit's very ordinary brown suit. She smiled. Cratchit's *threadbare clothes had been brushed up to look sensible* once again. He had filled out, so it fitted better now, but the plain, almost shabby coat was still loose across the shoulders.

Her heart melted. "Mr Cratchit, I believe? You are looking well," she said quietly. Just saying that made her realise something. Her relationship with Cratchit had been as a nurse and patient. She was not here as his nurse... not anymore. "I have come, just as I promised."

"AT THE DANCE YOU ASKED ME FOR MY OTHER NAME / BUT I HESITATED / IT IS MAX / FOR MAXWELL / AND WHITAKER IS A NAME YOU ARE FAMILIAR WITH"

She nodded. "Pleased to meet you Mr Max Whitaker." She could say it now without swallowing. "Don't you think that is strange? Max could

142

be short for Maximillian. Perhaps somewhere, deep inside, I hoped that was you."

"YOU DON'T HAVE TO HOPE ANY LONGER / MIM WILL YOU COME FOR A WALK OUTSIDE"

"But Max, it is the middle of the night."

"YES IT IS"

"And it is dark." She remembered the same invitation, in this same room, an eternity ago. She hoped he would not back out.

"I AM BLIND / IT IS ALWAYS DARK / THERES A LAMP HERE IF THAT HELPS"

"Oh, okay.... But you must know, I am not dressed for a walk."

Max looked pensive. *"Oh, I wish I could see you tonight,"* he thought with a sigh, as he held out his hand. Mim quietly came around behind his desk and linked her arm through his elbow, guiding him down the corridor. How many times had they quietly navigated these hallways during the dark hours, to walk around the grounds. As they stepped down the ramp, Max quietly tapped, "WE TURN LEFT".

"YOU PROMISED NO GLASSHOUSE TONIGHT"

"I KNOW / I AM A MAN OF MY WORD"

They walked past the Glasshouse. The lights were on but only a couple of the groundsmen were there, sweeping the floor. They continued past the tennis court, down through the grove of large camphor laurel and liquid amber trees. The wind whispered through the leaves, and the barking owl, roof-roofed.

"ARE THE STARS OUT TONIGHT" Max asked.

"YES / SO MANY / SOME LIGHT CLOUD / A QUARTER MOON"

"I SEE THINGS IN MY MIND WHEN YOU DESCRIBE THEM"

"THE STARS LOOK LIKE THE SPECKLING ON MY DADS ENAMEL MUG / EVERY TIME I DRINK FROM THAT CUP I AM REMINDED OF OUR NIGHT WALKS"

"YOU ARE EVERYWHERE FOR ME TOO"

"I HAVENT BEEN THIS FAR INTO THIS PART OF THE GARDEN FOR A LONG TIME / I FOUND ANNA DOWN HERE A FEW TIMES WHEN SHE WENT MISSING" They stepped around the overgrown hedgerows, and Mim gasped. A half dozen small hurricane lamps, like the one she was carrying, hung from the trees. A light supper was on a very weathered picnic table. Out of the shadows, cast by the flickering lanterns, Rick stepped forward like a Maître-d', impeccably trained by his father. He poured some champaign. Anna moved into the light, and quietly started to play her violin.

Mim looked around. "Oh Max! This is so lovely! Much better than a crowded dance hall". She nodded to Anna and Rick, "Thank you for this. The lanterns, the supper... the music. This is perfect."

Max turned towards Mim. "MAY I HAVE THIS DANCE"

Mim smiled gloriously! "Oh yes, you may!" They danced by the light of lanterns, starlight, and moon light. The music was soft and wistful, blending with the chorus of crickets, cicadas and the rustle of leaves. "Oh Max, this is perfect."

He smiled, his hand caressing her back. "THE DRESS LIVES UP TO ITS REPUTATION / IT IS STUNNING"

"I WISH I COULD STAY HERE FOR EVER"

He chuckled. "APART FROM GETTING HUNGRY WE WOULD BE PERFECTLY CONTENT"

She sighed deeply and placed her head on his chest. "CONTENT HAS BEEN A LONG TIME COMING FOR ME"

"AM I FORGIVEN FOR MY GROSS NEGLIGENCE AND MISJUDGEMENT"

"I AM SORRY I REACTED LIKE THAT / I SHOULD HAVE TRUSTED YOU HAD YOUR REASONS"

"I ONLY EVER HAD ONE REASON" He paused in the dance and stepped back, and still holding her hands, he knelt to the ground. He had practiced this with his prosthesis over and over. "MIM YOU ARE MY REASON / YOU HAVE BROUGHT ME BACK / BACK TO LIFE / BACK TO FAITH / FAITH IN GOD / FAITH IN PEOPLE / FAITH IN HELPING / FAITH IN LOVE / I AM A MAN UNAPOLOGETICALLY IN LOVE / MIRIAM LILY HILLMAN WILL YOU MARRY ME"

Mim quietly knelt beside him in the grass. "I first met you as Max Whitaker; then case file 7285: then Maximillian Cratchit. I have called you Rochester and Knightly at times... and perhaps you fit all of these in some way. But you are not your name; you are you: it is you whom I love. I would be proud to be your wife, Max Whitaker. My answer is yes." As they held hands, her grip tightened firmly. "YES"

He grinned as he plunged one of his hands deep into the pocket of his jacket and pulled out a ring box and flipped open the lid. The ring inside was one of his cufflinks... mother-of-pearl, black onyx, and blue lapis stone, rimmed with a sparkle of diamonds, set on a fashionable gold filigree band. "I SAW YOU LOOK AT MY CUFFLINKS ONCE LIKE YOU HAD SEEN

THE CROWN JEWELS / THAT LOOK OF WONDER IS SOMETHING I WANT TO LIVE UP TO"

"Oh, it is so handsome – but..."

"BUT"

"Max, you can't break up your set of cufflinks."

"I CAN AND I HAVE"

"BUT YOUR DINNER FUNCTIONS / THESE ARE PART OF YOUR SUIT"

"THEY DONT GO WITH BROWN" He chuckled. "I CAN USE A SAFETY PIN / OR GET ANOTHER ONE MADE / DO YOU LIKE IT / IS IT TOO CORNY"

"IT IS PERFECT" She slid it on her finger and stared at it for a long time. "Absolutely perfect Max." She wrapped her arms around him, holding him close.

They stood to their feet and kissed under the flickering light in the night garden. They hadn't even realised that the music had stopped, nor that Rick and Anna had left. They sat together, sipping champagne, nibbling some of Marlie's wonderful desserts, holding hands and tapping into the wee hours.

They walked back towards the house, their hands linked together, Mim stared up at the stars. She was thinking that this was not like the familiar stories that she loved and had dreamed of. This wasn't like the books written by Brontë or Austin or Dickens, but a rewritten story – a story where the characters were speckled, like stars flung across the majestic night sky or a common enamel mug. The characters in this story were grand *and* bland, both qualities side by side... but still united. There was bold and fragile, strong and weak, and it didn't preclude them from holding each other always. Where hearts belong together – they can be resilient and united... even while wounded and weak. Where destiny is life, sharing all of these things. Grandfield was no longer a riptide that she wanted to escape... it was a book she wanted to keep reading, right up until the last page.

⌘ ⌘ ⌘

The end

Other books by this author

Matt's Boys of Wattle Creek

Maggie & Minotaur

Rose's Diary

Gems of Australia Series:

Sapphires of Hope

Rubies of Ambition

Emerald Dreams

Homes of Healing Series:

The Beachside Cottage

Petrea Downs

The Writer's Retreat

Guthrie's Lot Series:

A Spacious Place

A Level Path

The Crying Tree

Pioneers of Grace Series:

Time of Grace

Circle of Grace

Journey of Grace

Mask of Grace

Crucible of Grace

Sculpture of Grace

Bottlebrush Grove Series

Shadows in the Corners
The Ragged Edges
Scratches across the Surface
Cracks through the Core

Children's Book

The Bush Olympics.
The Great Fly Hunter

Non-Fiction

Reflections in the Bible – Daniel
Reflections in the Bible – Abraham
Reflections in the Bible – Elijah
Reflections in the Bible – Job
Reflections in the Bible – David
Reflections in the Bible – Elisha
Reflections in the Bible – Joseph
Reflections in the Bible – Kings of Judah
Reflections in the Bible – Nehemiah
Reflections in the Bible – Samuel